About Charlotte Phillips

Charlotte Phillips has been reading romantic fiction since her teens, and she adores upbeat stories with happy endings. Writing them for Mills & Boon® is her dream job.

She combines writing with looking after her fabulous husband, two teenagers, a four-year-old and a dachshund. When something has to give, it's usually housework.

She lives in Wiltshire.

**'I could do with a new approach, I'll admit,'
she said slowly. 'So how about we strike a
deal?'**

'Go on,' he said slowly.

'What I need right now is an adviser. To help me get my
article back on track. Someone who knows the world I'm
writing about and can give me a few pointers.'

He stared at her.

'You want me to help you trick some unsuspecting
millionaire into thinking you're a rich socialite?'

'In a nutshell, yes. But not in a direct way. I just want to
be able to ask your opinion on a few things, that's all.
Clothes, locations—that kind of thing.'

There was something so alluring about her—and it messed
with his body, not just with his mind. Her upturned face
was imploring, the blue eyes clear.

'I'm no threat to you. I honestly have no interest in
making trouble for you. And we're not that different. You
told me you started out with ideas above your station and
that's what I've got. I just need this chance.'

He looked into the pleading blue eyes. He must be mad.

Secrets of
the Rich & Famous

Charlotte Phillips

MILLS
BOON®

First published in Great Britain 2012
by Mills & Boon, an imprint of Harlequin (UK) Limited.
Harlequin (UK) Limited, Eton House, 18-24 Paradise Road,
Richmond, Surrey TW9 1SR

ISBN: 978 0 263 22851 9

Harlequin (UK) policy is to use papers that are natural, renewable
and recyclable products and made from wood grown in sustainable
forests. The logging and manufacturing process conform to the
legal environmental regulations of the country of origin.

Printed and bound in Great Britain
by CPI Antony Rowe, Chippenham, Wiltshire

*This is Charlotte Phillips's fabulous first book
for Mills & Boon®!*

*We couldn't be more excited about
this uniquely talented author.*

*Enjoy the fun, flirty attraction
between Jen and Alex and
keep a lookout for more titles by Charlotte,
coming soon…*

For my family, with love and thanks.

CHAPTER ONE

How To Marry A Millionaire In Ten Easy Steps
by Jennifer Brown
If you can't earn it, marry it!

Champagne receptions, exotic locations, sumptuous food and designer everything. This is the world of the rich and famous, but is it a world of hype? A rich façade which can be infiltrated by following a few rules, wearing the right clothes? Or is there more to snaring one of the UK's most eligible bachelors than a makeover and a pair of fake designer heels?

No rich man will look twice at a woman he believes to be after his money, so to fit into the world of the rich you must look as if you belong there. You must seem like his equal, as if you have money and a beautiful life of your own.

Join me on my undercover mission to find out if an ordinary Miss High Street like me, with a day job and a mortgage, can reinvent herself on a budget to join the world of the beautiful people and win the ultimate prize: the heart of a millionaire!

Rule #1: Move to the right postcode, even if you have to live in a shack

JEN BROWN stood rigid behind the bedroom door in the dark, arm raised, the vase in her hand poised to be broken over the intruder's head the second he entered the room. As the door swung open one last thought dashed through her mind before cold panic set in and impulse took over. She wished, not for the first time this week, that she was back in her mother's cottage in the country, where you could leave your door on the latch all night and still not be murdered in your bed.

A state-of-the-art security system and a massive front door was apparently not enough to guarantee that here in Chelsea.

As the door opened and the light snapped on she leapt with a yell from her hiding place and swung the vase with every ounce of her strength. If this were a movie she would have knocked him out with one crash and then waited smugly for the police to arrive and pat her on the back. But this was reality. And she wasn't movie heroine material.

And so it was that before she could connect vase with scalp, before she had the chance so much as to kick the man in the shins, she was soaring backwards through the air to land with a thump on her own bed. Her wrists were immediately held in an iron grip on either side of her head, and as the intruder loomed above her she drew in a lung-ful of air and screamed as long and as loudly as she could.

She surprised herself with how loudly, in fact. He recoiled a little at the sound, his face catching the light, and she realised with a flash of disbelief just who she was staring at. Last seen yesterday morning on the front of her newspaper, in the flesh he looked even more gorgeous but a lot angrier.

She'd just tried to crack the skull of the most influential figure in British film-making.

* * *

'Calm down, I'm not going to hurt you!' he shouted over her, exasperation lacing the deep voice.

Famous or not, he had her pinned to the bed, so she ignored him and began to suck in another enormous breath.

He took advantage of the break. 'Drop the damn vase and I'll let you go!'

His dark green eyes were just a couple of inches above her own. The sharp woody scent of his expensive aftershave invaded her senses. Hard muscle was contoured against her body as he used his legs to pin her down effortlessly. She struggled, trying everything to move her legs and kick the stuffing out of him, but she couldn't move an inch. The eyes looking into her own were determined, and his breath was warm against her lips.

Drop the vase? She gave it a split-second's consideration. If her hands were free and he tried anything she could grab something else and bash him with that. The place was full of heavy minimalist ornaments—she'd be spoilt for choice.

'Let me go first,' she countered. Her heart thundered as if she'd just done the hundred-metre dash. She held his gaze obstinately.

He made no move to release her but his voice dropped to a *let's-be-reasonable* tone.

'You've just tried to brain me with it. Let the vase go and then perhaps you'd like to tell me what the hell you think you're doing in my house.'

Fear slipped another notch as her mind processed that last sentence.

She should have known the only person who could get past the Fort-Knox-style security system in this place would be the person who'd put it there. And if it had been daylight instead of the dark small hours she might have listened to her common sense instead of turning the situation into a movie plot. No wonder the house-sitting agency kept their property owners' details confidential. She could imagine women queuing up round the block to get this gig. It would be a stalker's dream.

She'd built up a mental picture over the last two days of the person who owned this beautiful apartment: *rich, clearly.* You couldn't rent so much as a shed in Chelsea unless you were *über*-rich and/or famous. Preferably both. *Male, definitely.* Everything in the place was pared-down and masculine. Exposed brickwork, black leather sofas, expensive spotlights, vast flatscreen TVs. No task was left ungadgeted. *And single.* In her opinion there was a serious over-use of art featuring the naked female form. Jen couldn't walk past the huge painting in the hallway without being reminded that her breasts were on the small side and she had no curves to speak of. No, the only women who passed through this apartment were overnight guests with no say in the décor. She was sure of it.

She congratulated herself on her powers of deduction. She was in the wrong profession. Perhaps she should swap journalism for the police force.

Alexander Hammond. Film producer. Award-winner. Millionaire playboy.

She let the vase drop from her fingers. He followed it with his eyes as it rolled away, the look on his face thunderous, and the next moment she was free as he released her hands and stood up.

He straightened the jacket of his impeccably cut dark suit. A pristine white shirt was underneath, open at the collar and devoid of a tie. His thick dark hair was cut short. Faint stubble against a light tan highlighted a strong jaw. He looked as if he'd just stepped off the set of an aftershave commercial. One of those ones filmed in black and white, showing the hero on his way home at sunrise, a glass of champagne in one hand and the perfect woman in the other.

She suddenly realised how she must look, staring at him with her mouth gaping open from her position on the bed. Warmth rose in her cheeks and she snapped her gaze away from him, concentrating on scrambling to her feet with some measure of dignity. Unfortunately on the way up she caught sight of her appearance in the gilt mirror on the wall. One side of her hair was plastered against her face and neck and the other side resembled a bird's nest. Terrific. Add in the greying old shorts and vest she'd been wearing in bed and she wasn't sure she could feel any more insignificant in the face of his gorgeousness.

She made up for it by drawing herself up to her full height and fixing him with a defiant stare. After all, he was the one at fault here. There was a two-day-old signed contract on the massive kitchen table, detailing her right to be here.

'You're paying for me to be here,' she told him.

She suddenly caught herself running her fingers through the tangled side of her hair and folded her arms grimly. What was the point? It would take a damn sight more than a hairbrush to turn small-town Jen Brown into the kind of woman who would impress Alex Hammond.

'I'm what?' he snapped.

'Executivehousesitters.com? I'm here to provide that extra level of security against intruders.'

She searched his face and saw his sudden understanding in the exasperated roll of his eyes.

'By crowning me with my own vase? That was your best effort at security?'

So an apology was too much to expect, then. Typical

arty type. Everything had to be about him. Never mind that he'd scared her half to death.

'What did you expect, creeping around the place when you're meant to be out of the country indefinitely?' She could hear the beginning of temper in her own voice. 'I'm not meant to be some kind of vigilante security guard, you know. I'm just meant to make the place look occupied, that's all.'

Apparently he could hear her temper, too, because he held up a placating hand.

'About grabbing you like that,' he said. 'You were just on me before I had a second to think. I could tell as soon as I got through the door there was someone here, I just assumed I'd had a break-in.' He leaned over the bed and picked up the vase, turned to replace it on the dresser. 'Thank God you're just a house-sitter. My PA booked it up. She must have forgotten to cancel.'

'Cancel?' Her heart plummeted.

He glanced at her. 'There's obviously been some mix-up,' he said. 'Something's come up and I need to use this place at the last minute.'

No kidding, something had come up. Jen had seen the news coverage. She knew instantly where this was heading for her—right out through the door and back to her day job at the *Littleford Gazette*—and she wasn't about to take it.

The *Gazette*, from which she was currently on unpaid leave, was great as far as rural local newspapers went, but she didn't want to be reporting on welly-throwing contests and duck pond vandalism for the rest of her career. She had big plans. Everything was riding on them. And they started right here, in the Chelsea apartment she was passing off as her own.

Having somehow managed to land an internship at *Gossip!*, a huge-selling women's magazine, she'd spent the last three months there, working herself into the ground, soaking up every piece of information she could lay her hands on, living on a pittance in a Hackney bedsit and loving every second of it. As the three months had come to an end she'd pitched an article idea to the Features Editor and got the go-ahead.

An investigation into the millionaire lifestyle from the angle of an ordinary girl. With a twist. This article was her ticket to a permanent job—a job that could change her life—if she could just come up with the goods.

For years she'd had a nagging curiosity about the lifestyle of the rich and beautiful. Who wouldn't, with a father who fulfilled both of those things in spades? Unfortunately he was severely lacking in other qualities, namely those needed to be any kind of parent—although perhaps he reserved that ability for his legitimate children. Pitching an article whose main requirement would be to infiltrate that elusive opulent world had been a natural choice. She'd been wondering what her parallel life might be like since she was a kid. Now she had the chance to find out, and take a huge step forward in her career at the same time.

A career with a top-selling UK women's glossy, living in London, living the dream, or back to covering dog shows at the *Littleford Gazette*, circulation five thousand.

No contest.

She intended—*needed*—to do whatever it took to nail this opportunity, and no man was going to stop her. Even if he was Alex Hammond. And even if it meant fighting a little dirty. The only advantage of having a waste-of-space millionaire for a father was that she wasn't the least bit intimidated by rich men. Although rich, *gorgeous* men were slightly more nerve-racking…

'It's too late to sort it all out now,' he was saying. 'You can stay the rest of the night, then get your things to-

gether in the morning and be on your way. I'll get my PA
to smooth things over with the agency. No need to worry.
I'm sure they'll find you something else quickly.'

He spoke with the air of someone conferring a great
favour. To add to the effect he gave her a lopsided win-
ning smile that creased the corners of his eyes and made
her traitorous belly perform a backflip. She wrapped her
arms defensively across her body. Just because it worked
on the rest of the female population—didn't mean she'd
let it work on her.

He made a move towards the door, his back already
turned. No need to wait for her response, of course, because what he said always went. How kind of him to let
her stay the rest of the night. A whole extra four hours. The
bitter taste of contempt flooded her mouth, quickly followed by sheer panic. How could she complete her article
if she got kicked out? She *had* to stay in this flat.

'I don't think you understand,' she called after him,
working hard to stop desperation creeping into her voice.
'I have a contract. You have to give me a month's notice
to move out.'

He paused at the door. She waited. He turned back to
face her, a frown touching his eyebrows. There was only
one thing for it—she was simply going to have to brazen
the situation out.

'This house-sitting thing—it's not completely one-
sided, you know,' she said. 'I'm still paying rent. I'm here
until New Years. I've even put up the Christmas tree. You
can't just barge in and throw me out because the mood
takes you. I don't care who you are.'

She saw coldness slip into the green eyes, and a slight
inclination of his head acknowledged that she'd recognised
him. Good. Then he'd know she wasn't about to be starstruck into doing what he wanted. This was her big break,

and not even his dazzling looks and reputation could stand in the way of her dreams.

'I see,' he said. 'Of course I'll compensate you for any inconvenience, if that's what you're worried about.'

He thought she was after his cash? She shook her head at him in disgust. 'I don't want your money.'

Why was she even surprised? She knew the type of man he was. She'd known that type her whole life. And not one cell in her body would submit to his insulting assumption that he could simply swan through life buying whatever and whoever he chose, throwing money at anything that stood in his way. As if a man like him could ever understand her desperate need to prove herself on her own terms.

She sat down obstinately on the bed.

He looked down at her for a moment.

'We'll talk about this in the kitchen,' he said.

Alex Hammond glanced through the house-sitting contract which he'd found in full view on the kitchen table. It seemed she had a point. Two minutes later she walked in, barefooted, tying a dressing gown around her. It was short, and he couldn't help but notice the long, long legs and the dishevelled bed-hair that made her look as if she'd been doing something other than sleeping. He felt a spark of heat deep in his abdomen. A couple of weeks earlier and the surprise discovery of a scantily dressed woman in his apartment would probably have led to him trying to talk her back into the bedroom and giving her the one-night stand of her life. That wasn't an option now. As of this week, he needed to be a changed man.

That resolution would be a whole lot easier to stick to without those legs under the same roof as him.

She didn't sit down. Instead she lingered in the doorway watching him, leaning against the jamb.

'I don't want your money,' she reiterated. 'Not everyone can be bought, you know.'

He shrugged.

'In my experience they can,' he said. 'It's just a matter of finding the right price. Tell me yours and we can skip all this tedium, sort the whole thing out, and you can get on your way. Everyone can do with a bit of extra cash at this time of year.'

She shook her head stubbornly.

'I'm staying put. You're welcome to serve me notice, if you like. In fact, let's assume that's what you've just done, shall we? So I've got a month before I need to move out and at the end of that time I'll go. No arguments.'

He had to admire her persistence.

'I've had a look at the contract...' he glanced down at her name on the top sheet of paper '...er...Jennifer, and I can't see what the problem is. I'll make sure the agency finds you somewhere else to stay that's just as good as this, and I'm prepared to offer you generous compensation for the misunderstanding. What's not to like?'

'Somewhere else isn't good enough,' she said. 'It has to be here.'

A lightbulb flickered on in his mind at the desperation clearly audible in her voice. Was that it? She was some kind of obsessive fan? Oh, great. Just what he needed.

He tried to speak kindly. 'Listen, Jennifer, I know there's a strong fan base for my work, and I'm grateful for that, but you have to understand I like to keep my work life and my private life separate.'

More like *have* to, from now on.

He saw her eyes widen, and her lip curled a little. It occurred to him that for a fan she didn't seem particularly keen on him.

'This isn't about you!' she snapped. 'It's about the address.'

She wasn't making any sense. He felt suddenly very tired. Not surprising after the few days he'd had and the night flight in from the States.

'What's so significant about this address if it isn't the fact that I live here?'

She dropped her eyes from his, fiddled with the belt on her dressing gown.

'It's an important part of my cover story,' she said. 'I can't change it now. There's too much riding on it. And I only have limited time and means.'

Her cryptic explanations were beginning to irritate him.

'What the hell are you talking about? Cover story?'

'I'm a journalist.'

The words fell like rocks into his tired mind. He'd just flown thousands of miles to get out of the scrutiny of the press pack only to find that one of them had moved in with him. He fought to keep a neutral expression on his face, to hear her out, when what he really wanted to do was frogmarch her out of the apartment and lock the deadbolt behind her.

'What kind of journalist?'

'I'm working on an article that involves me inventing a different identity,' she said. 'The house-sitting is a cheap way of getting myself an address in the right...' she pursed her lips '...social bracket. I'm working to a tight budget.'

He tried again.

'What paper do you work for?'

The blue eyes cut away from his.

'I'm freelance,' she said.

So she worked anywhere and everywhere she could. Terrific. It was time to wrap this up—immediately.

'Get your stuff right now and leave,' he said. 'I don't

give a damn about any contract. My lawyers will take it from here.'

She tilted her chin up and looked down at him, as if another bargaining tool had suddenly occurred to her. 'Mr Hammond, you must know that with a couple of phone calls to the right people I could have paparazzi outside this flat before the sun comes up,' she said.

He saw steely determination in the blue eyes and braced himself against the surge of rage. These press people—thinking they could manipulate any situation.

'Are you threatening me, Miss Brown?'

She shook her head quickly.

'No, I'm not,' she said. 'You can believe me when I tell you I have absolutely no interest in what's going on in your life.'

She must be the only journalist in the country who didn't.

'I'm working on a very specific project. I don't want any trouble, and neither do you.'

'But you don't seriously expect me to move out of my own house?' he said. This was the best place for him to lie low, decide his next step. He certainly didn't intend to do it with anyone else under the same roof.

'I don't,' she said.

She crossed the room and stood on tiptoe to take a glass from one of the cupboards. The movement made her robe ride up, and he fought to take his eyes off the length of creamy slender thigh it revealed. There was something undeniably alluring about her in a scruffy kind of a way. She went to the water dispenser on the side of the fridge and filled the glass. Not a hint of awkwardness, acting as though she lived here and he was the guest.

'I'll be no trouble. Just imagine you've got a very easy to live with house guest until New Year. God knows the place is big enough for two of us without getting in each other's way.'

For some reason his mind snapped to the bedroom, to that lithe body pinned underneath his, the blue eyes gazing back at his own...

'And what if I refuse?'

She shrugged. 'I've got a lot invested in this. A girl has to make a living, and if you pull the plug on this article I'll have to find something else lucrative to write about.'

The pointed look she gave him said it all. Cross her and her next project would be him.

He'd heard enough.

'Pack your stuff,' he said. 'In fact, no—don't pack your stuff. Get whatever you need for the night and get yourself out of here. I'll have someone send your bags on. You can collect them from the house-sitting agency.'

She didn't move an inch. In fact, she got closer.

'You people are all the same, thinking you can do whatever you like just because you've got a huge bank balance. I have a legal right to be here.' Alex wasn't so tired that he didn't hear the desperate edge to her argument, but right now he *was* too tired to care.

'I don't get this,' he said, levelling his voice with conscious effort. 'I'm prepared to pay all your costs, cover any lost income. You could restart your project without losing anything. An address change can't make that much difference.'

She took a sip of her water and Alex noticed her hands shake slightly. *Good,* she must be feeling nervous.

But she still shook her head. 'No, thanks.'

'Why the hell not?'

'Because I've already set myself up with this address and I'm not screwing around with that. Plus I don't dance to anyone's tune just because they happen to offer me hard cash. I can get where I want to by myself, thanks very much. This way you get to keep a low profile...that *is* what you're doing here, isn't it?...and I get to finish my article. Everyone's a winner.'

She folded her arms. She looked as fresh as a daisy, clearly prepared to argue all night if necessary, and suddenly he was done with it.

'Stay the damn night, then,' he snapped. 'You'll be out in the morning before you've had your first cup of coffee.'

The words were barely out of his mouth before she made a move towards the door, immediately taking him up on it. She disappeared, her bare feet padding softly down the passage back to the bedroom.

He stared at the empty doorway. Let her have her victory. It would be short-lived. In a few hours' time his legal team would have it sorted and he could bolt the door behind her.

Alex switched the phone to his other ear and looked out of the bedroom window onto the square below. It was early and traffic was still light. A couple of hours' sleep hadn't soothed his mood and he was more on edge than ever. Mark Dunn had been his lawyer and close friend for a decade, providing confidential advice he trusted on a personal and business level.

'You're actually telling me I can't evict her from my own apartment? What is the law there for? There has to be some kind of loophole.' He gripped the phone between ear and shoulder so he could flick again through the house-sitting contract.

'Without looking at it I can't be certain, but these things are essentially rental contracts.' Mark's voice was matter-of-fact. 'Fax it over and I'll check it out. Of course you could insist she leaves regardless of what the contract says, but in the circumstances that might not be wise. What's she like?'

Young, slim, minxy blue eyes. Legs that shouldn't be allowed.

'Knows her own mind and is refusing to back down,' he said. 'Hinted that she could make trouble.'

'She most certainly could if she wanted to. Alex, think how this could look if she put the right twist on it. All this stuff in the press about you and Viveca Holt. It's just a few weeks until the awards season kicks off and, trust me, the words "casting couch" are not ones you want bandied about in the run-up to that.'

'You think I don't know that?'

The familiar bite of fury at the backlash resurfaced. How dared people dictate what he did? Who he chose to see? Part of him wanted to issue a statement: *Yeah, so I had a fling with Viveca. A great time was had on both sides, if I say so myself, and I doubt it did her career prospects any harm. But really it's none of your damn business.*

'You need to kill that story stone-dead,' Mark carried on. 'Listen to your PR team for once. You're paying them enough. Go to ground for a few days and then gradually start to be seen again on your own in the right places. Maybe a few carefully chosen public events. Be seen to be having a quiet Christmas away from the limelight. Regain some respectability. Don't give them anything to write about and it will all be forgotten by New Year. What you *don't* need is some loose cannon of a journalist getting a scoop on you assaulting your own tenant and then throwing her out on the street. And that's just one story she could come up with. There could be worse. These people aren't big on truth. Any new story will be used as an excuse to rehash this current scandal. It could run and run if you don't handle it right.'

Alex felt fury begin to mingle with extreme frustration. The last few days had been hell. The constant paparazzi attention had made work impossible, and then there'd been the backlash from the film studios backing the movie. He had no choice but to get things back on track if he wanted to limit the damage to his professional reputation. Since his business empire had been his one priority these last five years, he had no choice but to play the game.

'OK, so if throwing her out isn't an option, what do you suggest?'

'If I were you, while we come up with a solution, I'd let her be and do my best to keep her sweet.' He paused. 'Not *too* sweet, though, Alex. That's the kind of thing that got you into this mess.'

CHAPTER TWO

Rule #2: Get your eye on the prize. Before you can trap the heart of a millionaire you have to be able to identify him. To observe the visible signs that set a wealthy and eligible man apart from the rest of the dross you must observe him in his own environment.

THE kitchen was a vast cold expanse of gleaming cupboards and spotlights and stainless steel. Not so much as a pepper mill cluttered its surfaces. Its clinical sterility reminded her of a hospital, and Jen hated it more than ever this morning. No matter how hard she told herself that she was the exception to the female rule, absolutely *not* attracted to Alex Hammond, her subconscious wasn't getting the message.

The recurring thought of lying on the bed beneath him, his muscular body hard against hers, had invaded her mind and banished sleep for what had been left of the night. The residual adrenaline from facing down a furious Alex hadn't helped, either. As a result she was now edgy and tired, her relief at being able to stay in the flat short-lived. For the first time in weeks she longed for her cosy kitchen back home, with its threadbare sofa in the corner, perfect to curl up on if you shifted the cat to one side before you sat down.

There was no sign of Alex Hammond this morning. He

was obviously sleeping in after the late night. She listened hard for a moment to make sure…

Nothing. The perfect opportunity.

Kneeling down next to the stainless steel dustbin, she pressed the button on the lid to open it and scrabbled around, grimacing as she shoved aside teabags and egg-shells and goodness knew what. At last she found what she was looking for: yesterday's newspaper. She tugged it out, scattering coffee grounds across the glossy grey-tiled floor and smoothed it out with her fist. Folding herself up on the floor, she settled down to read the article she'd only skimmed yesterday.

Now she was sharing a flat with him she wanted every gory detail.

Unfortunately Alex's face in the photo was obscured by a blob of cold scrambled egg from last night's supper. And as she began to read the irony of that fact wasn't wasted on her. Since a costly divorce five years ago he'd been living the life of a rich bachelor to the full. And if you in-sisted on dating a different woman every week, all of them beautiful and most of them famous, it stood to reason that sooner or later one of those affairs would come back and bite you very publicly on the behind. It was a simple mat-ter of probability.

The latest film from Alex Hammond's extremely suc-cessful production company, *The Audacity of Death*, was already tipped to clean up at next year's awards season. Its star, the young and stunningly gorgeous Viveca Holt, had been plucked from obscurity to take the female lead role over a number of well-established actresses. None of this had mattered one bit until pictures had surfaced of Alex Hammond stepping out with Viveca during the film's pro-duction and the rumour mill had begun with a vengeance.

The glamour surrounding the film-maker and the film

star being together was far too good to pass up. Whether or not sour grapes were to blame wasn't clear, but the implication from the press pack was that Viveca had moved from obscurity into the role of a lifetime via Alex's bed, with him pulling strings along the way. Definitely *not* the kind of publicity a serious piece of arty film-making needed, with award nominations being announced next month.

Jen nearly hit the ceiling when Alex Hammond walked unexpectedly into the room. She frantically screwed the newspaper into a ball. He looked down at her as he rounded the corner, at the bin open next to her spilling its contents across the floor, and raised his eyebrows. She coloured.

'What are you doing?' He moved smoothly across to the counter and switched on the coffeepot.

She squashed the paper back into the bin and slammed the lid down on it.

'Recycling,' she lied, getting to her feet. She soaped her hands under the single curved tap in the enormous double sink. Conscious of his far too observant eyes still on her, she added, 'Everyone can play a part in saving the planet.'

Oh, yes, that sounded just *great*.

He was looking at her as though she were a moron, then he shook his head lightly, as if to clear it.

'Coffee?' he asked, coldly polite.

She smoothed her hair back from her face with one hand, drew in a composing breath.

'Yes, please,' she said. 'Black, no sugar.'

He opened one of the many cupboards and took out two mugs. She waited, wondering if he was going to pick up where she'd left off last night on the eviction thing, but he didn't mention it. He simply filled the mugs with coffee and handed one of them to her. Then he leaned back against the counter, mug in hand, watching her.

Even on a couple of hours' sleep he looked fantastic, it

was so unfair. His hair was still damp from the shower, and he was dressed casually—just jeans and a dark grey polo shirt that on its own probably cost more than her entire wardrobe. She folded her arms defensively across her own cheap white shirt and jeans and took a sip of her coffee.

'You checked my contract out with your lawyer, then?' she asked.

He grinned wolfishly. 'Of course I have.'

Of course. Men like him left nothing to chance. She wasn't the least bit surprised. She waited, ready to argue her point. He probably had the best lawyers in the world, more than capable of pulling apart a standard rental agreement, but she knew she'd touched a nerve when she mentioned the press even if it had been just a bluff. She was just a reporter on a small country paper, not a tabloid entertainment correspondent. Her last story before she'd started interning had been about a cat who'd hopped on the bus and travelled from Littleford to the next village all by himself. That was the level of celebrity she was used to dealing with.

He didn't say anything else, just carried on looking at her with that appraising expression in the green eyes which made her self-conscious no matter how hard she tried not to be.

'And?' she prompted, when he didn't say anything.

He sipped his coffee.

'While I *could* break the contract—and I'm sure the house-sitting agency would be prepared to be *reasonable* about it...' His tone made it obvious who he considered the troublemaker to be in this scenario. 'You've told me how important it is to you that you keep this address. And, as I'm all in favour of enterprise, I'm prepared to be the bigger person here and honour the agreement. I wouldn't want to make things difficult for you.'

She bridled a little at his taking the moral high ground but kept her irritation under wraps. She didn't believe a word of it. He needed to keep his nose clean. That much was clear from the newspaper article and his turnaround since last night. Any sniff of scandal and he'd be back on the front pages. She had no intention of going to the press—she just wanted to concentrate on her article, on not letting her big chance, her *only* chance, slip through her fingers—but she didn't need to tell him that.

Let him think she had the editor of every London tabloid on speed dial.

'That's really good of you. Thank you,' she said through gritted teeth.

He raised his mug in acknowledgement.

She waited until he began scrolling through his mobile phone.

'Will Viveca be joining you for Christmas?' she asked pointedly.

His expression as he looked up from the phone was dark and inscrutable. She saw a flash of the arctic coldness from the previous night.

'No, she will not!' he said curtly. 'It's a working relationship, nothing more.'

'That's not what the papers say,' she said.

'And of course they are always right about absolutely everything.' He slammed his mug down, slopping coffee across the granite counter. 'It was a few dates and it was months ago. Can't I go on a couple of nights out without the world reading God knows what into it?'

Clearly not. She would give him her standard live-in-the-public-eye-at-your-peril lecture.

'That's the thing, though. You're happy to court publicity when it suits you. When it's *good* publicity. When there's a film to promote. You can't then say it's unaccept-able when people want to know more about you.'

'Well, you would say that, wouldn't you?' he said. 'Seeing as you belong to the *vulture* camp. Hoping to get the scoop, are you? Well, there's nothing to scoop. I'm single. I only date when I have to, and I don't see that it's anyone else's business. There's a line between public and private. Who I date and why I date them is private.'

She gave her suddenly pricked-up ears a mental slap. The fact that he was single was definitely of no interest to her. She didn't care that he was utterly, heart-stoppingly gorgeous. Firstly, she'd be wasting her time. Even in a ketchup-smeared photo Viveca was nothing short of ex-quisite. He'd never look twice at someone like Jen. And secondly, the only circumstances in which she would look at a man who paved his way through life with his wealth would be false ones—as demonstrated perfectly by her un-dercover article. She wasn't about to repeat the mistakes her mother had made. No way.

She shrugged. 'You're just too newsworthy. That's the problem. You need to keep your head down a bit more. Perhaps if you dated someone a bit more run-of-the-mill for a change?'

He raised his eyebrows and gave her a suggestive grin that sent a curl of unwelcome heat through her body. 'Someone like you, you mean?'

The kitchen felt too warm. The look in his eyes took her right back to the previous night again.

'I don't consider myself to be run-of-the-mill, actu-ally,' she said.

She felt his eyes follow her as she crossed the kitchen. She could tell just by the heat in her cheeks that her face was currently approaching tomato-red. No way was she letting him see that he affected her. She opened a stainless steel door and stuck her head into the cupboard where she'd stashed her food. She took a few calming breaths and when the flustered feeling was gone took out a loaf of bread.

She'd done a big supermarket food shop during a fleeting visit home a couple of days ago, left half the food in the house for her mum and brought the rest back to London with her. She had enough on her plate here trying to track down millionaires without also having to track down budget food.

She put a couple of slices of bread into the gleaming toaster. His attention was back on his phone again as he leaned against the counter.

She hauled her mind back on task. Sparring with Alex Hammond was all very well, but she needed to concentrate on work.

Thankfully, her accommodation remained sorted. She mentally ticked it off. Now for the next step. Somehow she needed to work out how the hell a girl whose most expensive item of clothing was a fifty-pound pair of shoes could identify whether a men's jacket cost a hundred pounds or a few thousand pounds? She needed to build up a sketch of the kind of man to target, and she had to admit there was a certain satisfaction in the idea of fooling a man of her father's ilk. Someone driven by money and reputation and success, who held all the cards in life and had no qualms about playing them.

Her first proper undercover expedition was tomorrow night. OK, maybe she was running before she could walk—she hadn't even got her wardrobe together yet—but a ticket to the first night of an art exhibition had fallen into her lap via the middle-aged arts correspondent of the *Littleford Gazette*. It turned out boring Gordon was a real culture vulture in his spare time, hanging around galleries and getting himself on exclusive mailing lists. When he'd heard about her planned article he'd thrown a spare ticket her way. She suspected he had a bit of a soft spot for her and feared he might expect a bit more than a cream cake as a thank-you if she had to go back to work at the *Gazette*. There was a lot riding on this project in more ways than one.

The opportunity to attend a champagne reception which would undoubtedly be *stuffed* with rich singletons was too good to pass up. If nothing else she'd be able to observe, and if she was really, really lucky she might be able to highlight a couple of suitable men to target. She hadn't had time to source any designer clothes yet. Instead she was intending to wear her trusty little black dress and blend into the background—use the evening to get an idea of the image she needed to build for herself.

But the thought of going straight from comfort zone to such a glossy affair was terrifying. She somehow needed to ease herself into it. A bit of people-watching would be just the thing to get her in the right mind-set. But knowing where to start was the problem. Where *did* the beautiful people hang out in London on an average week-day?

A sudden movement from Alex made her glance around to catch him checking the huge gold watch on his wrist—probably worth more than her car. Somewhere in her mind a penny dropped.

Standing in front of her was a walking, talking information source on every aspect of the lifestyle of a wealthy single man. Unfortunately with a messy and very expensive divorce in his past he was unlikely to see the funny side of an article on landing a rich bachelor, no matter how tongue-in-cheek it was meant to be. She'd have to find an underhand way to tap the information out of him.

He looked back up at her, a questioning frown knitting his brows in response to her sudden beaming smile.

'Would you like a slice of toast?' she asked him.

Ten minutes later they were seated on stools next to the granite counter. Alex watched Jen finishing her second slice of toast. A few crumbs clung to her full lower lip and he found himself staring at them until the movement of her hand as she brushed them away snapped him out of it. He gave himself a brisk mental shake. He was meant to be keeping on her good side, not ogling her. Mindful of Mark's warning to keep her sweet, he'd only agreed to the toast to appear friendly after snapping at her about Viveca. He surreptitiously pushed the remains of it to one side of his plate and took a large slug of coffee.

He looked up at her to see that she'd finished eating and was now staring at his wrist. She leaned forward on her stool to get a better look.

'That's a lovely watch,' she said.

He smiled distantly. What was she up to now?

'Thanks.'

'Would you mind if I took a closer look?'

Before he could answer she'd jumped down from the stool and taken a step closer. She took his wrist in her slender hands and turned the watch this way and that, examining it.

'Cartier…' she murmured.

He realised that she was the perfect height for him right now, standing next to him as he sat on the stool. This close he could see the big blue eyes, the frown touching her brows lightly. The curve of her top lip above the full pink lower lip was adorable. There were fine tendrils at the nape of her neck where she'd pulled her light brown hair up from her shoulders into a messy ponytail. He was reminded suddenly of the last time he'd been at eye level with her—last night, with her slender wrists in his hands, lush body pinned beneath him on the bed, close enough to kiss her with one short movement of his head. Heat sparked on his skin at her touch and seemed to pool deep in his abdomen.

This was not a good sign. Less than four days since he'd sworn off women and he was mentally wondering what she might taste like. He debated for a moment if he should have ignored Mark's advice and evicted her, anyway.

He tugged his wrist away sharply.

She looked up in surprise, her hands left empty in mid-air.

'I've got a conference call in twenty minutes that I really ought to be preparing for,' he lied.

She took a step back, still eyeing the watch.

'OK, not a problem. I'm planning on going out, anyway, so you can have the place to yourself.'

Honestly, she had more front than Blackpool. Acting as if she was the one doing *him* the favour when it was his own damned apartment.

She tossed his cold toast in the bin and stacked their plates together in the sink.

'Can you recommend somewhere good for lunch?' she asked, her back to him. 'I need to get a bit of background on the area. The kind of people who hang out here, what they wear—that kind of thing.'

He shrugged. 'Depends what you're after. Coffee and a sandwich? Or something a bit more substantial? What do you want to spend? Some places are pretty exclusive and expensive.'

She turned back from the sink in time for him to see the sudden shadows in her blue eyes.

'Not that I'm implying you'd be out of place there,' he

said, wondering why he was worried about hurting her feelings.

'Why don't you just tell me where *you* would go?' she said. 'If you were hypothetically going out for lunch in South-West London.'

He thought for a moment, trying to come up with somewhere she might enjoy.

'La Brasserie,' he said. 'French-style place. It's very popular—decent food.'

'Great, thanks!'

'Don't thank me until you've tried it. We might not like the same kind of food.'

She left the room. Just as he was insisting to himself that she was having zero effect on him he realised he was watching the graceful way her legs moved in the slim-cut jeans. He'd have to find a way of getting her out of here.

The globe lights, the ceiling fans twirling above her, the framed French posters on the walls and the marble-topped bar made stepping into La Brasserie feel like stepping into a little corner of Paris in the middle of London. Strings of white fairy lights and Christmas greenery added a warm festive touch. At a corner table, Jen thought it really was the perfect place to while away an hour or two people-watching.

She glanced at the menu and drew in a quick breath at the prices—even after her internship they never failed to amaze her. The coffee shop back home in Littleford did a knockout shepherd's pie for a fraction of the price of the main lunch menu here. Then again, the residents of Littleford wouldn't know what to do with a place that served frogs legs in white wine and parsley, Coquilles St Jacques—whatever *that* was—lobster and steak tartare.

When a waiter in a pristine white shirt and black waistcoat arrived to take her order she chose only coffee and a *pain au chocolat*, with a pang of regret that she couldn't afford to sample the full deliciousness of the menu. She needed to eke out her money big-time if she wanted to frequent places like this and actually look as if she belonged. The group of young women having a girly lunch at the table opposite made her feel totally invisible. She was kidding herself, thinking she could pass herself off as one of them in her High Street wardrobe. She needed designer *everything*. And on the money she'd scraped together that was going to be no mean feat.

The women were glossy without being in your face. Hair loose and natural, with gentle highlights, perfect smiles, less-is-more make-up and not a hint of orange fake tan. Clothes impeccably cut. Fur seemed to be *the* accessory this winter. No outfit appeared to be complete without a bit of dead animal attached to it somewhere.

So this was the world her father inhabited, while she and her mother were an inconvenience he'd written off twenty-four years ago just by opening his wallet. She didn't think she'd ever had a stronger feeling of being on the outside looking in. Jen felt plain, boring, and like an impostor with her mousy brown hair and her cheap handbag. And the worst of it was that none of that should matter—not to her. But still it did.

Wasn't the whole point of her article to look at this world of luxury from the perspective of an ordinary High Street girl? Her fresh eyes would enable her to pick up on all the little things that stood out. Like the way people air-kissed both cheeks as a greeting. Jen had never done that in her life.

She was furious with herself. She was an investigative journalist—a professional gathering background for an article. She should be finding this interesting, not intimidating. But try as she might she couldn't quite squash the needling little voice in her head reminding her that if things had been different, with a shift in circumstances, this could have been *her* world, too.

Darkness was already filtering in as she left the restaurant, and the cold air burned her cheeks, but she forced herself to do a bit of window-shopping on Brompton Road instead of skulking back to the apartment. In the brightly lit Chanel store, with the interlinked Cs logo huge behind an exquisite suit in the window, she could feel the eyes of the perfectly groomed assistants following her in her cheap jeans as she picked up a black tweed jacket—heavy in her hands, impeccably cut. Beautiful. She checked the label and felt the moisture disappear from her mouth. Maybe if she sold her car. And then some.

She put the jacket back slowly, so as not to look as if she couldn't afford it, more as if she'd decided it really just wasn't *her*. And she checked out a couple of handbags and a scarf on her way to the exit in an attempt to leave with some dignity. None of the staff approached her, clearly knowing perfectly well that she wasn't worth attending to. She wasn't the real deal. And all the while she was thinking that what she really wanted was to be back in sleepy Littleford.

She snapped herself out of it. She was just a bit homesick. It wouldn't last. These last three months in London had gone by in a whirl and she'd loved every pacy second of it. Christmas in Chelsea exuded class. It was all twinkly white lights and mistletoe, co-ordinated colours and not a tasteless bauble in sight. It couldn't be further from Littleford, which by now would have its threadbare Christmas tree put up on the village green by local volunteers. The same balding tree had been resurrected every year for as long as Jen could remember.

She wanted to stay in London and this was her chance
to do that. Her chance to show she could claw her way up
in life by herself. She didn't need a rich father smoothing
her path for her.

An hour or so later and things were looking up. It was
amazing what people sold online. She scrolled through
the auction listings on her laptop, propped up comfort-
ably against the pillows on her bed, mug of hot chocolate
next to her. It was gobsmacking how much of a discount
you could get for pre-owned clothes. No time to wait for
the auction to unfold over a week. She concentrated on the
'Buy Now' options.

Within half an hour she'd been possessed by a kind of
madness. It was all too easy to click 'Pay Now'. A pair
of jeans, a wear-anywhere shirt, a stunning velvet cocktail dress and a heavily knocked-down pair of nude shoes
that she hoped would go with everything—all by design-
ers she'd only ever read about in upmarket women's magazines. She snapped her eyes away from the screen and
calmed her racing pulse with the fact that she could sell
the whole lot on when the project was over with.

Before she could stop herself she'd clicked 'Pay Now'
on a gorgeous leather tote bag. In for a penny, in for…a lot
of pounds. Hmm, it was just too easy to get carried away
online when the clothes were this delicious. She'd better
do a quick recce of the cost. Her wallet was under serious
strain. She'd ploughed her meagre savings into her project—after all, you had to speculate to accumulate—but
still she needed to watch her spending.

The cost of renting the apartment, although seriously
discounted from what it would *really* be to rent a place
like this, was still taking up the lion's share of her budget. Add in the anticipated cost of tickets, entry fees, food

and drink—all the essentials she needed to actually get herself in the same room as her prey—and she had hardly anything left for her own makeover. And, judging by the young women she'd seen today, she was in serious need of one of *those* if she was to pass herself off as one of *them*.

She tapped the figures into her pocket calculator and stared in disbelief at the total. Clothes alone would never be enough, she needed to look the part inside and out. That meant hair, make-up, fake tan, nails. How the hell was she going to manage all of that on the ten pounds twenty pence she had left in her budget?

'Sorry, could you just say that again? I thought you said you were sharing a flat with Alex Hammond, but that can't be right, can it?'

'You didn't hear me wrong.'

Jen held the phone away from her ear with a grimace, but still the piercing squeal of excitement was audible. When it came to overreaction, Elsie was a professional. Then again, to someone who'd spent a lifetime living in Littleford, and for whom the working week consisted of giving perms and blue rinses to the village's pensioner contingent, the news that your friend was living with a celebrity was probably the highlight of the year. When the squeal subsided she tentatively put the receiver back to her ear.

'Are you sure?' Elsie asked breathlessly. '*The* Alex Hammond? The one on the front of today's newspaper with no shirt on? I've never seen abs like it.'

Jen made a mental note to check out today's paper, then mentally crossed it out. She didn't have time to think about Alex Hammond's abs. She felt mildly offended by Elsie's disbelief. Was it really *that* far-fetched that she could move in these social circles?

'Yes, definitely *that* Alex Hammond,' she said.

Elsie sighed.

'So any chance of you coming home before Christmas Day is even more non-existent, then? I'm dying of boredom here without you. What's he like?'

'Nowhere near as hot in the flesh,' she lied.

She hadn't counted on Elsie being quite so starstruck. It was a good few minutes before she could get her off the subject of Alex's physique and onto the subject of the favour she needed to beg. For Pete's sake, her future career was at stake here.

'I need your help,' she said when she could get a word in. 'The success of my article depends on it.'

She'd bored Elsie rigid with her writing career plans since they'd both been at school.

'What kind of help?'

'I need to look like a goddess—on a budget and in minimum time,' she said. It sounded an extremely tall order spoken out loud.

'How long?' Elsie asked.

'One day would be nice. For a start, is there some over-the-counter product I can use to make my hair look sun-kissed?'

Elsie made a dismissive chuffing sound.

'Pah! You don't need to bother with any of that over-the-counter rubbish. Not when you've got a professional on your team. I'll see you right. Don't you worry.'

'But you're in Littleford. And I can't afford to pay for you to come here even if I was able to let you stay.' She didn't bother to enlighten Elsie about the fight she'd had to keep herself under this roof.

There was a disappointed sigh at the end of the phone.

'I suppose it was too much to hope for a meeting with Alex,' she grumbled. 'And it's been ages since I've seen you. The place has been dead quiet since you took that magazine job.'

Jen squashed the sudden pang of homesickness. No matter how much she had missed her, Elsie would eat Alex alive if she got within touching distance of him.

'Sorry,' she said apologetically. 'He's rarely home, anyway. We barely see each other. And even if you *were* here, what I'm after is that modern, subtle, glossy-but-undone look the It-girls have. I need to look like myself, but better. I'm not sure there's much of a call for that kind of look in Littleford.'

She was trying hard to be tactful but clearly failed, because Elsie gave a derisory sniff.

'A couple of months in London and you think we're all hillbillies,' she complained. 'Just because I spend my days doing shampoo and sets for grannies doesn't mean I don't have all the skills for modern stuff, you know. A tint is a tint, whether it's blue, pink or just-back-from-Cannes-gold. I'll pop some colorant in the post tonight, shall I?'

Jen brightened immediately.

'Is it something I can do myself, then? Can you write me a list of instructions?'

'I can do better than that, honey. I'll instruct you *personally* via Skype.' She spoke in bossy and professional tones, as though she were a stylist to the stars, then ruined it by adding with a touch of stalker, 'Now, give me Alex Hammond's address.'

After a day of catch-up phone calls and e-mails, in which the subject of his swift departure from the States was skated over, Alex wandered into the kitchen on a fact-finding mission. Mark's follow-up phone call had come that afternoon.

'There is no Jennifer Brown that my press contacts

have ever heard of, but it's hardly an unusual name, and the world is stuffed with freelancers trying to get a foot in the door. If anything that makes her more dangerous. She's getting exclusive first-hand experience of your day-to-day life, and at some point—if it hasn't already—it will occur to her that she's sitting on a fantastic scoop.'

The morning papers had brought another spate of articles about him and Viveca, and Alex's never hugely impressive patience was close to breaking point. There were three films in varying stages of production that he should be immersed in, and instead he was stuck here, keeping out of sight, all because the studios backing them financially were unsettled by the sudden tabloid interest in his sex life. At this time of year more than ever he wanted to be busy. *Needed* to be busy. Working hard and partying harder. Anything but sitting here twiddling his thumbs in the flat with time to think about what might have been. He just wanted this whole ridiculous thing wrapped up so he could get back to doing what he did best.

'Then get something on *her*!' he snapped at Mark. 'Get some leverage that we can use if she tries anything.'

'I can't do that when I don't know who she is,' Mark protested. 'I need more background. Though it fills me with dread to say it...' he took a breath '...you're going to have to go and chat her up.'

CHAPTER THREE

FINDING the kitchen deserted, Alex followed the sounds of the TV and found Jen in the small den off the kitchen. It was a small, informal sitting room, cosier than the vast main lounge, with a small sofa, a couple of chairs and a very inferior forty-inch TV set. Where television was concerned, in Alex's opinion, size definitely mattered.

Jen was curled up in the corner of the sofa under a well-worn patchwork quilt that he didn't recognise. In fact, glancing around, he saw quite a few items that couldn't possibly have been put there by the interior designer he'd employed. There were framed snapshots and Christmas cards on the sideboard, tinsel on the mantelpiece and a small potted Christmas tree near the window. A fire crackled in the grate.

From nowhere came an unexpected flash of envy. She'd settled in. Surrounded herself with things that meant something to her, reminded her of her home, her family. When had he last done that anywhere? When had he last bothered with Christmas decorations? These days it didn't seem worth the effort just for him, although Jen clearly didn't see it that way. Home for him was whichever house he happened to be in, and family didn't fit in his life any more. Susan had seen to that.

Jen was wearing glasses and eating cheese on toast from

a plate that was balanced precariously on the arm of the sofa. She looked tiny and somehow fragile.

She glanced up at him.

'Hi,' she said.

He nodded towards one of the empty chairs. 'You mind?'

She shrugged noncommittally, but turned the sound down on the TV and took her glasses off, so he figured she couldn't be dead against him joining her.

'I thought the whole appeal of the executive house-sitting thing was that people get to experience luxury they can't afford themselves,' he said, settling back in the chair. 'You know—get a fabulous pad at a fraction of the rent.'

She was watching him, blue eyes wide. He liked the way she didn't fuss with her appearance. Her hair was piled up in a messy bun and he could see a tiny spray of freckles over her nose. No evidence of hours spent in front of the mirror with a make-up brush. He was used to ultra-groomed women, for whom venturing out was all about the way they looked. She was a breath of fresh air.

'What's your point?'

'So how come you're eating cheese on toast off your lap in the den? The sitting room doesn't look lived-in, and you didn't even bag the master bedroom. This is the only room apart from the kitchen that looks like you've set foot in it. You *are* free to use the whole apartment, you know.'

'Where would you suggest I eat, then?' she asked. 'That enormous glass table in your dining room? The one that seats twelve?' She shrugged. Smiled faintly. 'I'm not that kind of girl.' She glanced around. 'I feel more at home in here. It's cosy. You can keep your huge lounge with that monster TV.'

He felt another uncomfortable twist of nostalgia as for no reason his childhood home slipped into his mind. Not a glass table in sight back then, and they'd been lucky to have one temperamental old television. But Jen had sparked his interest with her indifference to the luxury trappings of the apartment. If anything it seemed more of an aversion. Yet hadn't she said her article was something to do with the opulent side of living in South-West London? Time to charm it out of her.

'Do you want a coffee?' he asked.

When he came back with two mugs she'd finished her toast. The empty plate was on the table.

'How was today, then?' he asked, sitting down. 'What did you think of La Brasserie?'

She held her cup in both hands, like a child, and smiled up at him.

'It was amazing,' she said.

'Did you get the background you were talking about?'

She shrugged. 'I got some,' she said. 'You should have seen the food! There were things on that menu I've never even heard of, let alone tried. And the people were something else. I wanted to get an idea of image, you know? What the young women in the Chelsea set are wearing, how they act.'

Her face became animated as she talked about her project. He felt absurdly touched by her excitement over a restaurant he'd visited more times than he could remember. Over things he no longer noticed.

'And what did you think?'

'I think I've only seen the tip of the iceberg. I mean, there were quite a few touristy types there, too, but it was still an eye-opener. They're all so glamorous. Fantastic clothes! One girl had a dog living in her handbag!'

He burst out laughing and she tentatively smiled back. As the blue eyes lit up he realised she was quite stunning.

Good thing he had Mark to keep him on task. She could be a serious threat to his newly sworn singledom if he let her.

'Where do you live usually, then?' he asked. 'When you're not staking out the Chelsea set? I thought it must be somewhere in London—you know, at the journalistic hub?'

Jen paused for a moment to collect her thoughts. It was one thing to share an apartment with the guy, another to start telling him personal stuff. Then again, she could do with some leverage here. This morning's recce had given her some good ideas about working on her own image—and now she'd got Elsie on board to help with hair and make-up, and hit the online secondhand shops so hard that the thought of it still gave her palpitations.

What she was lacking was information on the type of man she was aiming this image towards. She had no personal experience in that area. Her mother had always avoided talking about her father at all costs, never refer-ring to him without using a variety of colourful expletives. La Brasserie hadn't really been much help there, either. Wealthy businessmen were apparently too busy making themselves richer to be chilling out in the daytime mid-week—no matter how posh the restaurant, and no matter how delicious the food.

Speculate to accumulate. Maybe if she made small talk with Alex she could get some tips out of him and distract herself from the still lingering sense of isolation her af-ternoon's research had left her with.

'I've been in London for the last few months, but really I'm from Littleford,' she said. 'It's a small village in the West Country. You won't have heard of it.'

No one ever had.

'Not far from Bath?'

'You've been there?' she said, wondering when the hell

he'd have had the need to drop in to a village where the star social attraction of the year was the Farm Festival in July, when everyone got together to admire cows and stuff themselves with local produce.

He shook his head. 'No, but I know the general area quite well.'

When she looked at him expectantly he added, 'I grew up in Bristol.'

'You're from *Bristol*?'

'You make it sound like the moon.' The green eyes looked mocking. 'I haven't always lived like this, you know. My parents are working class. My dad was a lorry driver and my mum was a dinner lady at my school. I could always count on her for extra custard.'

'Really?'

'Your surprise could be construed as insulting, you know,' he said.

'I guess I just assumed you'd had a…well, a privileged upbringing.'

'Why? Because someone from my background couldn't possibly make something of themselves?' His tone was light, but the eyes had a razor-sharp edge to them.

She backtracked. *Hard.*

'I didn't mean that. It's just…well, it's such a glamorous career, what you do. Hollywood, London, Cannes.'

He shook his head.

'I didn't have any of that in mind when I started out.'

He took a sip of his coffee. She waited for him to elaborate, but it seemed his own glam world wasn't as interesting to him as it was to her.

'What's Littleford like, then?' he asked.

'Quiet. One pub, couple of village shops, church, duck pond,' she said, trying to fob him off quickly so she could get the subject back on him. 'So, how did you start out?'

Her plan to pump him for background information on what suits he wore was trampled underfoot by her stampeding curiosity about his childhood. She'd assumed he'd been born to wealthy parents and had had an upbringing involving public school, nannies and a network of contacts that had given him a leg-up until he'd reached the top. Just how wrong had she been?

'I started out small,' he said. He looked down at his coffee mug, a smile touching his lips, creasing the corner of his eyes lightly. 'I guess I just always had big ideas.'

She smiled at that but he shook his head.

'It wasn't particularly a good thing. Where I lived you got through school, then you got out and started earning. Big ideas were seen as a waste of time. I had to fight to get my parents onside about going to college. I worked part-time to fund the course, but there was a real sense that I was wasting that money. I was lucky. I had an inspirational tutor and I was determined to succeed. I made a short film. Just a twenty-minute thing I wrote, produced and directed on a minuscule budget. I knew it was good. I believed in it totally.' He laughed a little. 'Feature films came much later. Ideas above my station never really went away.'

'Nothing wrong with that,' she said. She could definitely relate to it. 'You don't get anywhere by sitting around.'

She realised suddenly that she was feeling hugely impressed by him, and quickly reminded herself that he might have made his own wealth but he didn't seem to be in touch with his roots now. Typical. Get there and never look back. He obviously wasn't above using his money to ride roughshod over other people now he'd got it.

'So you live alone?'

He asked the question casually, without meeting her eyes. The kind of question that might be asked on a date. A spark tingled its way up her spine at the thought and she felt mildly ridiculous. The idea that Alex Hammond might be interested in someone like her when he could call up a model at the drop of a hat was ludicrous.

'With my mum,' she said.

A sudden stab of longing for home made her forget momentarily she was meant to be on a fishing expedition. Try as she might she couldn't really feel at home in this apartment. She was looking forward to going home for Christmas, but she couldn't think past her article right now.

'It's just the two of us. She lost her job recently, and I've been interning, so things have been a bit tight money-wise. I'm hoping this article comes off because it has a great job riding on the back of it. If I can up my earnings, she can slow down a bit.'

An alternative, if their backs were squashed any harder against the wall, *had* been floated. She could contact her father and tap him for a handout—as suggested often by Elsie, for whom pride had no value in the face of hard cash. For Jen it was out of the question. She'd prefer to be poor with her pride intact, thank you very much.

'So you're in the market for lucrative stories, then?' Alex asked.

She didn't miss the suspicious look on his face. Understanding flooded in. A friendly conversation? She knew immediately what this was all about.

'You're wanting to know if I'm planning an exposé on you, aren't you? Is that what this being friendly is all about?'

'I'm just making conversation.' His voice was totally calm.

She put her mug down on the coffee table and pulled herself up from the sofa. She shoved aside an almighty twinge of disappointment. What an idiot she was for thinking he might actually be interested in her and her country background. He was a stereotypical bachelor with enough cash to get his own way on anything he chose. He must be super-nettled by the idea of her living here to go to the trouble of trying to sweet-talk her. Well, good. As long as she didn't have to move out, let him be nettled.

'I told you last night—I've got no interest in you as long as I'm working on this project. As long as you're not planning on throwing me out you have nothing to worry about. Your secrets are safe with me.'

'You don't know any of my secrets.'

She walked around his chair and leaned in behind him, laid a hand on his shoulder and bent down to speak in his ear in what she hoped was a confident *I-won't-be-messed-with* tone. She'd seen it done in the movies, when Mafia bigwigs wanted to be intimidating. Unfortunately she wasn't prepared for the sudden happy flip-flops in her stomach that the scent of his warm skin and expensive aftershave would cause, and she had to talk through gritted teeth to keep up the charade and stop her voice slipping towards soft and melty. That would definitely have ruined the effect.

'I could always make up what I don't know,' she snapped, dropped the TV remote control in his lap and stalked out of the room.

As she made her way to her bedroom she forced herself to focus hard on her article. She wasn't going to get anywhere with the research questions now. She'd just have to wing it at the exhibition tomorrow with no head start at all.

Rule #3: Don't forget...etiquette! If you're going to join the world of the rich, you must act as if you belong there. Blending in isn't just about what you wear—it covers how you speak, what you say, your manners. Do not swear, get drunk, do drugs or laugh loudly. Avoid flashy behaviour. You are aiming for girlfriend to be swiftly followed by wife. Not mistress. Stand out for the wrong reasons and your cover will be blown.

It felt like getting ready for the scariest night of your life. A cross between a first date and a job interview pretty much covered it. Jen told herself the nerves were down to the fact there was so much riding on this project—nothing to do with the feeling that she was a fraud, that she didn't belong in this world. She had a perfectly good reason to be there: research. And this was her first real opportunity to mingle with the kind of men who thought nothing of blowing the odd million pounds on a painting.

In fact, there wasn't an enormous amount of stressing over what she was wearing. She only had one remotely suitable dress with her. None of her online purchases had turned up yet. She was still in serious need of a make-over. No millionaire worth his salt was going to look twice at mousy-haired Jen Brown in her High Street LBD and shoes, but at least she could stand on the sidelines and learn to identify the kind of man she should be targeting.

There would be no point changing her own image if she couldn't tell the difference between real money and an ordinary culture vulture like Gordon from the *Gazette.* She needed to nail the difference between bespoke tailoring and mass production. She felt a bit more positive. This wasn't going to be a wasted evening. It was going to be a dry run. A learning experience.

And, talking of learning, she had nearly an hour yet before her taxi was due. What would be a more productive use of that time than a bit of investigation? Alex Hammond might not be up for twenty questions, but this apartment was full of the trappings of his rich life, just there to be examined. She padded down the passageway from her bedroom in her stockinged feet. Alex had been out for most of the day and had shut himself in the study the moment he got back. There was no sign of him emerging any time soon.

She stopped outside the door of his dressing room and hesitated. Dressing room? Honestly! What kind of a man needed one of those?

The kind who had so much hard cash he didn't know what to spend it on, she answered herself, pushing the door open. A little look wouldn't hurt. She was sure he wouldn't mind.

There were dark wood sliding cupboards on either side, a tiled area with his-and-hers smoked glass sinks, and a gleaming mirror took up almost the whole wall at the end of the room. The lighting was unforgiving, and she grimaced as she caught sight of her pale complexion in the mirror. She really would have to get some fake tan sorted out if she wanted to look as if she regularly holidayed in the South of France.

Sliding open cupboards, she was faced with rows of perfectly cut jackets, pristine shirts in every colour, and racks of gleaming shoes stored with wooden moulds inside them. She picked up a pair and studied them. Italian leather. She could see they were beautifully made, but she could hardly spend the evening staring at men's feet. She decided to concentrate on the clothes instead.

She reached into the wardrobe and took out what looked like an evening suit in a very dark slate-grey. She unzipped the transparent dust cover and took the jacket off its hanger. She examined it, trying to burn the look and feel of it into her mind. The fabric was rich and heavy, the cut so sharp that it even looked perfect hanging from her hand.

On impulse she shrugged herself into it, just to see

what it might look like on a person. It smelled faintly of the warm citrus aftershave Alex wore, snapping her straight back to the first time she'd breathed in that scent. The jacket, huge on her, reminded her of the breadth and strength of his toned shoulders as he'd held her down, his green eyes locked on hers. Her breathing speeded up just at the thought of it, and she could see in her reflection the pink hue that rose in her cheeks. She wished her body would get the message that she didn't have time for men like him. Not when she'd spent her whole life grappling with the reason why a man like him had no time for her.

She was turning this way and that, examining the fall of the jacket in the mirror, when the door opened behind her and Alex Hammond stepped into the room.

She felt as though her heart had fallen through the pit of her stomach.

His hair was damp from the shower and he was wearing a sea-green bath towel around his hips, to which her eyes traitorously dipped before she got herself under control and dragged them back up to face level. The toned pecs and biceps were lightly tanned. He looked as if he'd just stepped in from the beach.

For a long moment Alex couldn't quite believe what he was seeing. Hot on the heels of yesterday's thinly veiled threat to make him her next story, now he found her standing next to the open door of his wardrobe, apparently trying on his clothes.

'I can explain,' she said.

At least she had the good grace to look embarrassed. The blush high on her porcelain cheeks made her look very young, and prettier than ever.

This would be interesting.

'Cross-dressing?' he supplied helpfully.

Without looking at him she took the jacket off, hung it back on the hanger, zipped the cover over it and replaced it in the wardrobe. While her back was turned he crossed the room to stand behind her. This close, he was enveloped by her perfume, something light and sweet that knocked his senses. The skin of her shoulders, visible above the boat neckline of the dress, was the colour of double cream against the plain black fabric. Her neck curved delectably. He crushed the impulse to kiss it.

'First you go through my bin and now I find you looking through my clothes,' he said in a low voice.

She spun round, and he heard the small gasp as she realised how close he was to her. He saw in the surprised widening of her eyes that she thought she'd got away with the bin story.

'What the hell is going on here? What are you? Some kind of stalker?'

She stood her ground defiantly, looking boldly into his face. The confident don't-care exterior didn't fool him. He could tell by the way her breath had quickened, the way her eyes met his, that she was attracted to him. She thought she could blag her way out of this, as she did everything else.

'I came in to use the mirror,' she said. 'There isn't a full-length one in my room. And then I wondered if there might be a jacket I could borrow. I only have a pashmina and it's freezing outside.'

'Make a habit of wearing men's clothes, do you?'

'Masculine tailoring is the new black, actually,' she said airily. 'I was just having a try-on. It's a girl thing. You should never trust the way it looks on a hanger.'

She sidestepped him deftly. He let her go, watched her as she pretended to look in the mirror, dabbing her lips with her little finger as if trying on menswear was the most normal thing in the world for a girl to do.

'Naturally I would have asked your permission before I took it.'

'Naturally,' he said sarcastically.

She glanced at him.

It was clear now that she had to be gathering background for some article or other about him. He was shocked to realise how disappointed he felt by that. He'd begun to like her, with her off-the-wall behaviour and her amazing legs. He was used to mixing with women who played the game his way. A couple of dates, a good time, and when he broke it off—which he always did—they left on good terms. No fuss or backlash. Because his good opinion counted in the competitive world of film.

A woman with her own agenda was a refreshing change. And that was not necessarily a good thing.

He considered walking her to the door right now and throwing her out, but he needed to speak to Mark first. Make sure he'd found out something to ensure her confidentiality. That, he insisted, was the only reason he didn't tell her to go and pack now. It had absolutely nothing to do with the way she was affecting him from the waist down.

Obviously tasting victory when he didn't say anything further, she made for the door while the going was good.

'Going anywhere special?' he called after her.

'It's a work thing,' she called back. 'Don't wait up.'

The gallery would have been stunning even without pictures festooning the walls, Jen decided. The building itself was cutting-edge modern, and inside there was major use of glass, highly polished wood floors and superb clear spotlighting to show the art off to its best advantage. At least it would have done if any of the pictures had been Jen's cup of tea. Enormous arrangements of Christmas greenery studded with tiny white pin lights stood near the entrance. Wine waiters mingled effortlessly among the guests, dispensing crystal flutes of champagne and canapés. The artist was up-and-coming and, according to the loud-voiced man dominating the group next to Jen, extremely collectible. The guests were glamorous, their enthusiasm for the exhibits bubbling like the champagne.

Feeling drab and invisible in her plain black shift dress, and unsteady in her borrowed nude heels, she took a third glass of the complimentary champagne from a passing waiter. OK, so she rarely drank, but in this intimidating fish-out-of-water environment at least it gave her something to occupy her hands. She found herself sipping from the glass in an effort to appear busy and avoid speaking. Not that anyone had attempted to start a conversation with *her*.

There were plenty of extremely attractive men in attendance, but they seemed to have at least two or three women keeping them company at all times, all of them beautiful and expensively dressed. A few weeks to go until Christmas and sequins and gold were everywhere. The only way she'd be able to compete might be by tipping her champagne down the designer-clad back of the competition, and that would only get her ejected from the premises before she could so much as speak. Deciding the only way to salvage the evening was to treat it as a serious scouting mission, she chose the least offensive of the eye-wateringly bright oil paintings and picked her way through the crowd to stand on the edge of the group in front of it.

'Fabulous brushwork. So *insistent*,' one woman was saying to no one in particular. Her gold silk sheath dress screamed expensive. Not a hint of tasteless sparkle, more a subtle hint of *luxe*. It made Jen, in her boring man-made-fibre black, want to slink under the nearest rock.

She took a sip of champagne and gazed up at the picture. These people—honestly! Could they not see what was plain as day? To Jen it looked as if a toddler had run amok with a paintbrush.

Confidence shored up by the champagne, she leaned in towards the man standing next to her.

'Not sure about it myself,' she said.

Hah! She'd made a comment. Not so hard, after all! She took another slug of the delicious champagne and glanced sideways at him to see if he was listening. Hmm. Sleek blond hair, haughty but attractive face. Her eyes dipped expertly to his suit. Definitely expensive tailoring.

He smiled and nodded at her. He took a sip from his own glass and his sleeve fell back to reveal his watch.

Cartier!

It was like a message from the gods. She gave him her full attention.

Her confidence was soaring on the back of three glasses of champagne, and she realised with a flash of inspiration that this was the answer to all her problems. Dutch courage! She grabbed a passing waiter by the arm before she missed out, and swapped her empty glass for another full one.

The rest of the group drifted away, but the blond man carried on looking appraisingly at the framed paint explosion in front of them.

'Personally...' Jen leaned in conspiratorially and, extending a finger from the hand encircling her champagne flute, jabbed it towards the picture '...I like what I like. It needs to speak to me on a sentimental level.' She clasped her other hand to her chest to emphasise how heartfelt an opinion that was.

Oh, the champagne was marvellous. And she was just *so* witty and interesting.

'Tell me, what do *you* think of it?' She pasted an expression of interest on her face. Her high heels seemed strangely unsteady and she concentrated hard on not swaying.

The man began an extremely dull monologue on the inspirational brushwork, and she tried valiantly to listen and nod encouragingly when her will to live wanted to dash to the exit and throw itself under the nearest lorry. She glanced around for the wine waiter.

'…name?'

She suddenly realised he'd stopped talking and was looking at her expectantly. The chatter in the rest of the room seemed to have degenerated into a humming background noise.

Name. Right—she'd prepared for this. Something that sounded as if she'd been born into money, because she'd read somewhere that was more respectable than *nouveau riche*.

'Genevieve,' she said. Her tongue felt strangely hard to control.

'Genevieve?' the man asked.

One of her heels suddenly dipped to the side, and she plummeted four inches before managing to right herself by grabbing his sleeve. Champagne slopped from her flute onto his lapel. As she managed to steady herself he pointedly disengaged himself from her grip and took a step backwards, wiping at his suit. People around them began to look over at the disturbance, and she smiled around at them reassuringly—just a little accident, nothing to worry about.

'Genevieve?'

She glanced round at the voice behind her in confusion.

Next thing she knew she was being taken firmly by the elbow and Alex Hammond had control of the situation.

'Genevieve! I wondered where you'd disappeared to!'

His voice was loud and commanding. 'Excuse us...' he added in an aside to the blond man.

She suddenly found her hand encased firmly in his and his arm slid strongly around her waist, propelling her at a stumblingly fast pace towards the exit. Many more heads turned. Interested faces passed Jen by in a blur. As they descended the stone steps onto the frosty street the icy cold air hit her and made her head spin. She was vaguely aware of a crowd moving towards them, saw cameras and mobile phones raised as people clocked just who it was she was in a clinch with.

She struggled free and put a pace between them, intending to swing round on her heel and give Alex a piece of her mind. She didn't care what media grief that might cause him. She'd had it with his interference. Even though her knees went buckly and he caught her again around the waist, before she could hit the frozen pavement, she refused to let him get away with this.

'What the hell do you think you're doing?' She snapped crossly. 'I was well *in* there!'

CHAPTER FOUR

ALEX managed to hold his tongue until they were out of earshot of the press. Having rushed her into the safety of the back of his car, he had his driver head back to the apartment.

'Well in there?' he said through gritted teeth, wondering why he was so angry. 'That was not a school dance and you are not fourteen. Do you realise you just threw champagne over Viscount Dulverwell?'

To his utter amazement, instead of looking ashamed or embarrassed, she actually looked even more pleased with herself.

'Hah! A viscount, eh? I knew it! The watch gave it away.' She hiccupped suddenly and clapped her hand over her mouth.

His lips quirked. The sooner he got some black coffee into her the better.

'Anyway, why are you so annoyed?' She jabbed a finger at his chest. 'What were you doing there? Are you checking up on me?'

'No, I am not!' he snapped in exasperation. 'I'm being seen in the right places. Looking respectable. Looking *single*. And escorting a drunk young woman off the premises was definitely *not* part of my plan.' He glanced sideways at her, taking in her delectably dishevelled state. 'You'd better hope no one got a picture.'

He imagined for a moment the fallout if the chaos of the last fifteen minutes made it into tomorrow's papers. His PR team would have him becoming a hermit next. But suddenly Alex realised none of this made him the slightest bit regretful. If anything, absconding from the dull exhibition, rescuing a delightfully out-of-her-depth Jen, felt like a small victory in the face of the ridiculous media manipulation supposedly taking place on his behalf.

'Why do it, then?' she asked him.

'Do what?'

She gave an exaggerated shrug. 'Why escort me anywhere?'

She leaned in towards him, putting a slim hand on his arm and enveloping him in the vanilla scent of her perfume. His pulse kicked in response, hard.

'Why not just ignore me, let me get on with my evening while you do whatever it is you people do at these places? Buy one of those ghastly pictures, maybe? I didn't ask you to drag me out of there. I was managing perfectly well by myself.'

Thrown by his body's instant reaction to her touch, he plucked her hand from his arm and moved it back into her own personal space.

'I was saving you from making a total fool of yourself,' he said. Not strictly true. The sensible thing would have been to leave her to her own devices, keep as much space between them as he could.

He refused to acknowledge how he'd felt on spotting her across the gallery. At first he'd assumed she was there watching him, convinced as he was that she was now planning to write some story about him. But a few minutes' observation had made it obvious she hadn't a clue that he was there. Intrigued as to what on earth she was doing there on her own, he'd been unable to concentrate on the pictures or the conversation. His eyes had kept dragging themselves back to where she stood, nervously fiddling with her handbag, not speaking to anyone.

He'd seen how her confidence had grown in proportion to her champagne consumption. Watched her grow louder and more animated. And finally he'd watched her throw herself at Viscount Dulverwell, gazing raptly into his face as he talked, only breaking her focus on him to grab yet more champagne. For some reason watching her start out nervous and unspoilt, as if she were at her first grown-up night out, and slowly morph into a vivacious flirt had bothered the hell out of him. Whatever her reasons were, whatever she was doing there, he hadn't been prepared to wait until the end of the evening for an explanation.

Back at the apartment he took her firmly by the shoulders, marched her through the kitchen into the den and deposited her on the sofa while he made industrial-strength black coffee. The silky feel of her shoulders under his hands had him wondering if she felt that satiny all over. He crushed the thought from his mind. Maybe the fact she'd drunk too much was a good thing. If he were to pursue that impulse he would want all her wits and senses at his disposal.

Not that it was even a possibility.

While he waited for the kettle to boil he skimmed an e-mail Mark had sent while he was out. When he came back she'd kicked off the skyscraper heels and pulled the pins out of her hair. It fell in soft waves to her shoulders. She looked suddenly very vulnerable and he curbed the temptation to snap at her.

He sat down opposite her and leaned forward.

'I want to know exactly what is going on. What you're

really doing in London. Why you're in my flat, snooping in my cupboards, and why you were at that reception tonight by yourself. You tell me everything or I put you in a taxi right now.'

'You can't do that,' she said defiantly. She sipped her coffee and grimaced at the strength of it but didn't complain. 'You don't know what I might say to my press contacts.'

He held that defiant blue gaze unwaveringly with his own.

'Which contacts do you mean?' he asked. 'The one who runs the agricultural desk? Or maybe Births, Marriages and Deaths? They're standard fare in a village newspaper, aren't they?'

Mark's e-mail had given full details of her current employment. No tabloid newspaper contacts in sight.

Silence for a long moment, with the blue eyes fixed on his. Then she looked down at her coffee cup.

'You checked up on me,' she said accusingly.

'You turn up out of the blue, living in my apartment and refusing to leave, no matter how much money I put on the table. Not to mention all the weird stalker stuff. Did you honestly think for one second I wouldn't check up on you?'

He didn't add that he checked up on everyone these days, no matter how insignificant they seemed. Trust seemed to have been phased out of his life since Susan had left. After five years it was all but gone.

Jen took another sip of her coffee, pushed her hair back from her face. Her expression was steadier when she looked back at him. Sobriety seemed to be slipping back.

'I'm sorry about the weird stalker stuff,' she said. 'I'm not, in fact, a weird stalker.'

She paused and he waited for her to elaborate, waited to

see if she'd feed him another line or actually come clean this time.

She took a deep breath. 'I'm working on an article I pitched to *Gossip!* magazine.' She searched his face.

He raised mystified eyebrows.

'It's the biggest-selling women's magazine in this country,' she explained. 'I managed to land an internship there for the last three months, and at the end I pitched my own idea for an article.'

The look on her face was disbelief mingled with delight.

'I still can't believe it,' she said. 'I've been trying for the past three years to break into mainstream women's journalism but it's so damn competitive. There's a permanent job vacancy there and the editor said if I can pull this off I've got a great chance of landing it. A proper career. Not just an internship. This is my big break—my foot in the door. Christmas is my deadline, I have to file my copy by then.'

'And how does trying on my clothes and flirting with Viscount Dulverwell fit in to all this?'

She took a breath.

'My article investigates whether it's possible for an ordinary Miss Nobody...' she glanced up at him '...someone like me...to reinvent herself and win the heart of a millionaire.'

He stared at her, wondering if he'd actually heard correctly.

'Obviously a rich man with half a brain wouldn't look twice at me normally, because he'd assume someone like me must be a gold-digger, right?'

A sick feeling rose in the pit of his stomach as Susan flashed into his mind again.

'So I need to give the impression that I have money and success of my own. An address in the right postcode, the right clothes, the right things to say.' She took a sip of her coffee. 'And the right places to go. That's why I was at the exhibition. And that's why I've been taking a bit of an interest in your clothes and your lifestyle. I would have asked you outright but I didn't think you'd take kindly to the idea, given…well, given…'

Incredulity mingled with outrage. *Given the fact that the one person I trusted, wanted to spend my life with, turned out to have pound signs in her eyes and not a lot else…*

'Given my past, right?' he said.

Not for the first time he felt a surge of fury that his private life was public property.

'You mean to tell me you're posing as some socialite so you can bag a rich man? I've never heard anything so ludicrous!'

'It's not *real*. I don't really want to "bag a rich man", as you put it. Personally I'd rather eat my own head than get involved with someone like that.'

Even in his amazement he didn't miss the venom in that comment, and wondered where it had come from.

'It's a way of writing about that whole rich, sumptuous world without it just being a run-of-the-mill description. The editor of *Gossip!* wouldn't have wasted a second on me if I was just writing a straightforward article because that's been done a million times. The way I'm doing it is more fun. It gives an original spin. It's intended to be tongue-in-cheek, not serious.'

'Well, it's never going to work. I can tell you that now. You think a few new clothes and hanging out in the right places is enough?'

'*You* were there, weren't you?'

'What?'

'I said, you were there. Tonight. According to a recent poll you are the thirty-sixth most eligible bachelor in England right now. I checked.'

She'd been checking up on him? His mind zeroed in on that piece of information. He would revisit it later.

'What's your point?'

'That in order to meet a wealthy, eligible man you have to go to the right places. And I did. I just…drank a bit more champagne than I should have.' She rubbed a hand tiredly across her forehead. 'I'm not really used to it.'

'I think the whole article idea is laughable,' he said shortly.

She leaned forward and spoke slowly and clearly. 'It's a tongue-in-cheek social experiment. It isn't serious.'

'Judging by this evening, the experiment isn't panning out all that well.' He felt an unexpected jolt of regret as he saw the look in her eyes. Clearly she wasn't happy with the way it was going. Question was, why the hell did he care?

'I'm not giving up,' she said, 'if that's what you're hoping. That I'll just throw in the towel, pack my bags and be out of your hair. I'm going to make this work, no matter what it takes.'

'Nice though it would be to get my life back, I wouldn't expect you to go quietly.'

And that was the whole point, really, wasn't it? He was used to maintaining absolute control over every aspect of his life, used to excluding anyone or anything that could take advantage of him. If he wanted something he went after it. If he didn't want something he found a way of avoiding it. His wealth and position made that entirely possible. And now his lack of control over this situation, over her, was driving him nuts. Well, not for much longer.

'I've got a proposition for you,' he said.

Interest sparked in her face. She sat forward, the blue eyes shrewd. The only sign of the champagne now was in the dark circles beneath them.

'A confidentiality agreement,' he said. 'You sign that

and I allow you to stay here for the month. Long enough for you to finish your insane undercover article.'

The leave-nothing-to-chance reliability of a signed agreement appealed to him. He'd long since learned from the mistakes of his past.

'A gag order?' Her tone was tinged with contempt. 'You want to control my freedom of speech?'

Had he really expected her to sign on the dotted line without a word of protest?

'It's nothing out of the ordinary. It's a standard contract. All my staff sign one as a condition of their employment.'

'I'm not staff. And *you* might consider giving someone else control over your life to be nothing out of the ordinary, but I don't.'

'We'll both benefit from it. I'm not asking you to cut your tongue out—you can write about any other damn thing you like except for me.'

He felt a stab of exasperation. Did she have any clue at all what it was like to be on the receiving end of the press pack? To go through the worst of times and have to elbow your way through photographers just to leave the house? And, when they couldn't get what they wanted from you, to have them hound your family? To read about private details of your marriage break-up in the papers, your heartbreak there in black and white for anyone to see?

He watched her staring into her coffee for a moment, deep in thought. Eventually she looked up at him, a frown touching her eyebrows.

'I could do with a new approach, I'll admit,' she said slowly. 'So how about we strike a deal?'

Mark would have insisted he halt the conversation right there, withdraw the offer and tell her to go and pack. But there was something about her defiant attitude that he couldn't help responding to. In spite of himself, it stirred

him. In more ways than one. To put his business interests first he had to curb his socialising. Yet solitude did
not come easily to him, and having her here would offer
some diversion. The question was whether that was a good
thing or not.

He put his coffee cup down and met her gaze.

'What kind of deal?'

She shrugged.

'I admit you might have a point about my press contacts.
I don't know anyone in the national press. But I could still
make trouble. It wouldn't take much for me to ring up the
entertainment correspondent of one of the daily tabloids
and give the inside story of my few days in your company
following your scandal.'

A counter-threat. He wouldn't have expected anything
less.

'So you understand where I'm coming from?' he said.

She nodded. 'And I'm prepared to sign your agreement
if you change the conditions. Your offer is to let me stay
here, but I'm going to ask for a bit more than that.'

He wasn't sure he'd ever met anyone who pushed their
luck so hard.

'Go on,' he said slowly.

'What I need right now is an adviser. To help me get my
article back on track. Someone who knows the world I'm
writing about and can give me a few pointers.'

He stared at her.

'You want me to help you trick some unsuspecting millionaire into thinking you're a rich socialite?'

'In a nutshell, yes. But not in a direct way. I just want
to be able to ask your opinion on a few things, that's all.
Clothes, locations, that kind of thing.'

He needed time out to think.

'I think it's a fair offer,' she added.

As she put her empty coffee cup down on the table he got to his feet and reached for it.

'I'll make some more coffee,' he said.

She grabbed his hand as he picked up her mug. Sparks of heat tingled through his wrist and zipped down his spine. There was something so alluring about her—and it messed with his body, not just with his mind. Her up-turned face was imploring, the blue eyes clear.

'I'm no threat to you. I honestly have no interest in making trouble for you. And we're not that different. You told me you started out with ideas above your station and that's what I've got. I just need this chance.'

He looked into the pleading blue eyes. He must be mad.

She took her hand back and he straightened up, made his way back to the kitchen, knowing that he should be ejecting her from the apartment right now.

She was right about selling her story. She could still make life difficult for him if she wanted to.

He had a choice. He could make her move out now, take a chance that any fuel she added to the scandal fire would be short-lived. Or he could go along with her crazy scheme, get the gag order in place and keep her here with him for the month. The inherent danger in that thought made his pulse-rate climb. He ignored it.

It burned that he was expected to toe the line of the studios, the management, to restrain his private life. After clawing his way up from nothing to get where he was, and having been knocked halfway down again by Susan, being held back in any way now was abhorrent to him. His one failed attempt at family life had been dissected and trampled on by the media. Living the high life was pay-back for that. He enjoyed spending time in the company of beautiful women, but he never let it get serious enough to have emotional consequences. Let them print that he was screwing this model, or that actress. He didn't care whether it was true or not.

Jen wanted him to spend a bit of time giving his opinion on clothes and the like? How hard could that be? With his social life reined in he'd have plenty of time on his hands. Let her stay here and work on her mad project. It would give him a few laughs if nothing else. And he'd far rather look at her long legs and big blue eyes than stare at these four walls.

He could tell Mark he'd secured her silence. No need to mention that he'd given in a little on the terms of the agreement. Or that he found the prospect of spending a month living side-by-side with Jen dangerously attractive.

He refilled their coffee cups and made his way back into the den. He stopped in the doorway. She was curled up in the corner of the sofa, brown hair spilling over the cushion, sleeping. His heart turned over gently. For a split second he toyed with picking her up and carrying her to her bed. And then the memory of the other night drifted back—the thought of her beneath him, his for the taking. He mouth felt too dry all of a sudden.

There was kicking back and there was recklessness.

He put the coffee down on the table and grabbed the hideous patchwork throw she was so attached to. He tucked it around her and left the room.

Every movement around the kitchen jarred Jen's aching head. She cooked dry toast, took headache pills, then sat on one of the stools and swigged orange juice. All the usual tricks for dealing with a hangover. If she was going to feel this grim at the very least she should have had the luxury of memory loss—the kind where you missed hour-long sections from the previous night as if you'd been abducted by aliens rather than drunk too much champagne.

The humiliation of being escorted from the exhibition by Alex played on a loop in her head. She'd tossed a drink over a member of the aristocracy. For a professional journalist she knew her behaviour had been pitiful. And the *coup de grâce* that really made her cringe? Collapsing in Alex Hammond's arms on the gallery steps. Her face burned just at the thought of it. That they hadn't been swamped by the gawping paparazzi was down to pure luck and Alex's super-fast driver. Clearly the press had been as surprised as she was to see him at the gallery, and the car had pulled away with seconds to spare.

As soon as her head calmed down she would go and pack. All hope was gone of his letting her stay here. The champagne might have given her the courage to propose they strike a deal, but that had been her big mistake. Alex Hammond would never stoop to negotiate with someone like her. He'd see it as a challenge to his authority. Men like him did what worked for them. He'd wanted rid of her from the moment he arrived and now he'd got his way.

Deep down it wasn't the leaving that was the problem. Yes, it would be a setback. She had a ton of designer clobber winging its way to this address. A pain, but fixable. No, the thing that really rankled was that he'd got what he wanted despite her best efforts. Another rich man letting nothing get in his way—especially a nobody like her. She knew she could sell a story about him, but she was in this for the long haul. She didn't want fifteen minutes of fame for a flash-in-the-pan exposé and a one-off payment. She wanted to make a serious career out of writing, and that meant maintaining journalistic integrity. What if she wanted to interview a celebrity at some time in the future? She would never be trustworthy if she sold Alex out now.

He had no idea what it had cost her to agree to the gag order. The only way she'd been able to stomach it was to throw in some terms of her own, to try and hang on to some control. Well, much good it had done. Was this what it had felt like for her mum when she'd been pushed into signing the piece of paper that had let her father buy his way out of her future? As if she was painted in a corner with no other option left?

She glanced up and her heart began to thud as Alex walked into the kitchen.

'Morning, Genevieve,' he said.

She flushed. He'd got what he wanted. She'd be moving out. She didn't need to put up with him teasing her too. She jumped down from the stool, grimacing as the sharp movement jerked her head, and made for the door.

'When do we start, then?' he called after her.

'When you said you'd need a few pointers, I didn't expect to have to read women's magazines,' Alex muttered, flipping through the pile of glossies she'd handed him with a dubious expression on his face.

They were sitting opposite each other in the main sitting room on the leather sofas, a roaring fire burning in the enormous fireplace. A low coffee table separated them, upon which was a jumble of her handwritten notes, magazines, photos and a coffee mug each.

She wasn't about to let him off the hook now. Initially amazed that he'd agreed to her request, she'd quickly forged ahead with her plans before he could change his mind, booking proper slots in his diary so he couldn't make excuses. This was the first—deliberately late that afternoon, so her hangover headache had had the chance to dissipate completely. She felt totally alert and focused again.

'I think it's important you understand the kind of article I'm pitching. It isn't some serious literary thing, it's meant to be light-hearted and fun.' She took a slug from her coffee. 'And, anyway, you should be thanking me instead of complaining. These magazines are an insight into the mind of the modern woman.'

"'Christmas party make-up for every skin-type..."' he read aloud. 'Very insightful.'

She ignored the teasing.

'I'm talking about the stuff on relationships, not the make-up column. Articles on what women really think about foreplay. How to decipher what he really thinks of you by studying his behaviour.' She jabbed her pen towards him. 'There's a whole underground conspiracy between those pages that men just aren't aware of. A sisterhood. A sharing of information that arms us against the wiles of the opposite sex. Did you know that the majority of women at some point fake orgasm?'

'The minority who sleep with me don't,' he said.

Sparks tingled up and down her spine as he deliberately and firmly held her gaze, the heat clear in his expression. She picked up another of the magazines and began to flick through it, not seeing the content, just using it to deflect the moment. It didn't help that she knew exactly what it felt like to have his body held hard against hers. Without conscious effort her mind wasn't above taking that scenario further step by step. What it might feel like to be kissed by him, touched by him. She wasn't about to let him play with her the way he undoubtedly played with all the women in his life. She knew his type. What possible interest could he have in someone like her, besides amusement?

'Men have magazines, too, you know,' he said, apparently giving up on getting a reaction from her. 'Women don't have the monopoly on this stuff.'

She flapped a dismissive hand at him, glad to be back on task.

'You can't possibly compare lads' mags with the serious issues covered in women's magazines. They're just an excuse to show pictures of scantily clad women with the odd article about cars and football thrown in.'

'Nothing wrong with that,' he said, grinning.

He wasn't going to take this seriously, was he? She should have just launched straight into the stuff about image. Gathering up the magazines, she stacked them in a pile under the table and picked up her notebook.

'There's two areas where I need your input,' she said, keeping her tone efficient. 'Firstly, background on the kind of men I'm writing about. It should be easy. Just tell me about yourself. Where you go to socialise, what you wear, what subjects interest you, what sports you like—that kind of thing.'

He leaned back on the sofa, arms behind his head.

'You want to know about what makes me tick?'

The question was loaded. She could feel it. It made her stomach feel soft and squiggly.

'In as much as it relates to my article, yes,' she said, trying to keep her focus.

'And the other area?'

'My own image,' she said. 'I've ordered a stack of second-hand designer clothes. I just need you to give me a thumbs-up or down as to whether or not they would do it for you.'

'*Do it* for me?'

She felt heat rise in her cheeks. This would be so much easier if he was middle-aged, short and dumpy. It was hard to keep things businesslike with him looking like an Adonis. She didn't relish the thought of asking his opinion on her looks, but she was determined to give her absolute all to this article. She was more than capable of crushing any stupid embarrassment in the interest of the bigger goal.

'Make me look like I'd fit into your social circle without standing out,' she rephrased. 'Like I have plenty of money of my own.'

'Got you,' he said. 'I assume that's what the name-change was about, then, Genevieve.'

He seemed determined to keep a blush on her face.

'You have to agree that Jennifer Brown doesn't sound rich.'

'You could double-barrel your surname,' he suggested. 'What about adding your mother's maiden name?'

'Brown is my mother's maiden name.'

'OK. Add in your father's name, then.'

'I've got to twenty-five without using anything of his. I'm not about to start now,' she said, more forcefully than she'd intended. The fact that her father's name could open doors had only made her even more determined not to use it. She was determined to prove that money and string-pulling weren't the only way to get where you wanted in life—something Alex Hammond could do with remembering.

He raised his eyebrows but made no comment.

'Street name?' he said. 'Add your street name to your surname.'

'That would be Farmer-Brown.'

He burst out laughing and she couldn't help grinning back. He looked absolutely heartstopping when he laughed. Maybe if she got to know him she could talk him into giving her an interview somewhere down the line.

She marvelled at herself. Here she was, country mouse Jen, career-building and networking without even thinking about it.

'Maybe it's a sign. I think I'll just forget the name thing for now and concentrate on the way I look and speak. Having a name like a princess isn't going to convince anyone if I look and sound like trailer trash.' She frowned. 'Not that I do.'

'Sounds like a good idea,' he said. 'And next time you might want to lay off the champagne.'

CHAPTER FIVE

Rule #4: Get the right look. Don't be yourself. Be better. Walk better. Dress better. Groom yourself better. Ditch High Street for designer but avoid labels that show. Think simple, understated, classy. Get a decent haircut and colour and keep make-up subtle but pretty. On a budget? Trawl internet auction sites, or try charity shops in rich locations, for second-hand clothes and put together an expensive look that's versatile enough for different occasions...

'ARE you sure this will have worked?' Jen asked dubiously.

'Relax. It'll be a piece of cake. You followed my instructions, didn't you? You can't go wrong.'

Elsie's face, her hair in a new upswept bouffant style with a pink fabric flower pinned at one side, filled the screen of Jen's laptop. Alex was out for the afternoon and she'd taken over his dressing room. Mainly because there was a sink available and the floor was tiled, so any splashes of hair colorant would be easy to clean instead of carpet-ruining.

She'd stashed her laptop to one side of the sink unit and had mixed the colour under Elsie's virtual supervision before painting it onto her head. That had been a while ago and now it was time to rinse.

Alarm bells began ringing as soon as she began pouring jugfuls of hot water over her head.

'Er...Elsie?'

'Mmm?'

'Is the water meant to be this colour?'

Water the shade of what could only be described as fluorescent carrot swirled down the plughole, and she felt a pang of dread as she pulled the towel tighter around her shoulders and steeled herself to take a glance in the mirror.

Dark shock descended and she felt suddenly as if there was a brick in the pit of her stomach.

The aimed-for delicate shade of kissed-by-the-sun-blonde had turned out a rancid head-in-a-bucket-of-sick neon orange. Worse, the usually soft, silky texture of her hair seemed to have ended up somewhere between straw and candy floss.

Her reflection in the mirror gaped at her, lips pulled back from her teeth in a grimace of horror.

'Elsie, what have you done to me?' she howled.

Elsie put down her nail file and peered from the laptop screen.

'Oh, dear. That's a bit intense, isn't it? You can't have followed my instructions properly.'

'Don't you dare blame me for this! I've done everything you told me to do.'

'Perhaps it's the colorant,' Elsie said, pursing her lips thoughtfully. 'I know it had been lying around for a while but that shouldn't have made a difference. There isn't much call for sunkissed blonde in Littleford. Maybe it'll tone down a bit when it's dried. Mind you,' she added, 'it does look quite festive.'

So, under the guidance of her so-called friend, she'd just plastered her hair in out-of-date chemicals.

'Festive?' she yelled. 'The brief was myself, but better. Not *Sesame Street*!'

'What the hell is all the noise about?' Alex snapped irritably, banging the door open.

She saw the expression of annoyance on his face change to one of shock as he caught sight of her hair. She scrabbled frantically to hide it by throwing the towel over her head. Oh, please, not him—not now. Humiliation burned in her cheeks, turning them a shade of beetroot that clashed horribly with her new hair.

'Is that him?' Elsie squawked excitedly over Skype. Her face was suddenly enormous on the screen as she peered closer to the camera. 'Is that Alex? Oh, my God, I'm such a fan. You can't possibly imagine! Jen, could you budge to the left a bit so I can see him properly?'

Jen reached out in exasperation and slammed the lid of the laptop shut.

Alex stared at her, aghast.

'Who was that?' he asked. 'And what in the name of hell has happened to your hair?'

She burst into tears.

He took a step backwards.

'There's no need to cry!'

Livid with herself for making such a fuss, Jen unwound a large corner of the towel from her head and wiped it furiously over her face, swallowing hard to get herself under control.

'I've ruined everything,' she said, between snuffles. 'I might as well throw in the towel on the whole project right now. What's the point in wearing designer clobber when you've got radioactive hair? Looking like this, the only way I could trap a millionaire would be by drugging him. And it's all my own fault for thinking that someone who spends their days putting curlers in pensioners' hair could turn me into Viveca Holt!'

'Viveca?'

Why the hell had *that* particular name sprung to mind? There was absolutely no reason why she would want to look like Viveca. Alex would think this was some sad attempt to make herself attractive to him. She quickly flapped a dismissive hand at him.

'Figure of speech.' She clenched her hands in exasperated fury. 'Oh, if I'd just been a bit more restrained online this would never have happened.'

Clearly confused, he held up a hand.

'You're not making any sense. Calm down and tell me what's going on.'

She took a deep breath.

'I'm on a minuscule budget for my whole project,' she said. 'I've ploughed all my savings into it, but it isn't like I'm made of money. Every penny counts. I went a bit mad buying designer clothes online and realised I had hardly any money left for a makeover. Elsie agreed to show me how to do the whole lot for free,' she said, nodding at the laptop. 'Hair, make-up, nails, fake tan. Only I might as well have entrusted the job to Laurel and bloody Hardy!'

Her temper was on the rise again as her tears dried.

Alex pulled out his mobile phone and began scrolling through it. The bitter reality of what this meant hit home. The final straw.

'Oh, yes, go on—ring the lawyer again!' she said. 'I can't even blame you. Who needs this kind of chaos in their life? I think you'll find there's nothing in that agreement that says you can evict me because of comedy hair!' She raised her voice to a shout. 'I read the small print!'

Frowning, he held up a hand in a shushing gesture. She sank into a chair by the sink and put her head in her hands.

'Marlon?' he said into the phone. 'It's Alex. Great, thanks, and you? Good, good. Listen, can I arrange an appointment? Hair, make-up, styling, the lot. Soon as you can? We'll come to you. Sorry it's out of the blue but it's a bit of an emergency.'

Jen peered out at him from between her fingers, ears pricked up, heart suddenly racing.

'First thing tomorrow? Perfect!'

He hung up.

'Marlon?' she asked.

'Marlon Cobelli. He's the stylist I use when I'm shooting in London. He does a lot of work on my film projects. Bit of a drama queen but he knows his stuff. He'll soon sort you out.'

She saw his eyes dart upwards to the towel on her head. Hope rose as she realised what he was saying, only to be dashed again as the implications clicked into her mind.

'I can't afford London prices!' she wailed miserably.

He rolled his eyes in exasperation.

'I wasn't expecting you to,' he said. 'I'll throw it in with the accommodation. Call it a Christmas bonus—whatever you like.'

Her long-held principles held steady even against the current vile situation. Alex Hammond, cruising through life on a bed of cash. Well, she didn't *do* charity—she did it alone. She slowly shook her head even as her heart plummeted.

'Thanks, but I can't possibly accept that. I'll have to think of something else.'

Maybe she could sell something. She had some jewellery with her—not that it would fetch much.

'Why on earth not?'

'It's nothing personal. I just don't like to rely on other people, that's all.'

'You relied on Scary Laptop Girl.' He nodded at the computer. 'Why such a problem with me?'

'That's different.'

'How?'

'Because she's an old friend who owes me a favour. And you're throwing money at someone you don't even know.'

'But you've just said you'll have to throw the towel in. You'd rather do that, give up on your dream, than accept a bit of help?' His tone was incredulous, making her feel like a stupid amateur.

'This article's all about proving myself, showing that I can make my own success,' she said. She didn't want that principle diluted. She shrugged. 'I don't expect you to understand.'

He was watching her intently.

'Do you think the fact that I roped my friends into helping with my first film for free makes me any less of a success now?' he asked her. 'Or that I borrowed five hundred pounds from my college tutor to buy props?'

'That's different.'

'No, it isn't. It's fine to accept help sometimes. Everyone needs a friend.'

The expression on his face was unexpectedly sympathetic. It made her stomach feel soft and she felt tears approach again.

The fact obviously didn't escape him, because he gave an exasperated sigh. 'Oh, for Pete's sake. I'm under contract to help you with your image, aren't I? Terms negotiated by you in return for which you signed away your beloved freedom of speech. Just look at this as me delegating my responsibilities. Trust me, you'll do a lot better with Marlon on the case than you would with me. I mean, do I *look* like an expert on women's clothing?'

She looked down at her hands, thinking it through. It was this or hightail it back to Littleford. Back to covering country fêtes and dog shows. The thought filled her with despair. And what he'd said made her feel somehow less as if it would be accepting something for nothing. It wasn't a failure to take him up on it. Failure would be to go back. She slowly allowed blissful relief to bubble through her. Before she knew it excitement was back, and without thinking what she was doing she stood up and threw her arms around him.

'Thank you!' she said into his shoulder.

She was suddenly aware of his hand sliding around her waist in response. It sent simmering heat flying up her spine. And the delicious smell of his aftershave made a lovely replacement for the horrendous pungent odour of hair chemicals.

'No need to thank me. I'm doing it for me, really, not you,' he said over her head. 'I'm not sure I could face living with a Muppet for the next four weeks.'

The local hair salon in Littleford where Elsie trimmed Jen's ends every couple of months had a row of hood hairdryers along one side, a waiting room full of gossiping pensioners, a tin of traditional biscuits and a stack of years-out-of-date magazines on the side table. Jen couldn't help comparing it to the glossy mirror-lined walls and spotlighting of Marlon Cobelli's cutting-edge studio. A spiky black Christmas tree stood in one corner. The salon was clearly at the cutting edge of Christmas as well as everything else. It was a world away from anything she knew.

Jen's stereotype of a stylist to the stars involved someone impossibly trendy, bossy to the point of offensive and brutally honest in pointing out things like saddlebags and bingo wings. In pre-emptive self-defence she pasted a don't-care expression on her face and clung to the hope that he would also be the polar opposite of Elsie when it came to styling skills, and this hideous embarrassment would all be worth it.

Marlon turned out to be all of these things. He was also camp as Christmas, and greeted Alex with a smacking kiss on both cheeks. She noticed Alex returned the embrace without an ounce of self-consciousness.

She couldn't help feeling a touch of admiration. Now, *there* was a man who was comfortable with his sexuality. Her ex-boyfriend Joe, who worked as a farm hand and who'd put up with her for six months—a personal relationship best—would have deepened his voice and launched into a football anecdote before running a mile.

'This is Jen,' Alex said, pushing her forward and holding her there, as if he could sense she wanted to bolt back into the background.

The firm slide of his hand around her waist as he stood just behind her made her stomach flutter with more than just nerves. He was close enough for her to pick up the scent of aftershave on warm skin. She swallowed hard and tried to focus her attention on the stylist.

Marlon wore a slim-cut shirt with a flower print over skinny black jeans, and his shoes had the sharpest toe-points she'd ever seen. His eyes widened in surprise as she removed the baseball cap Alex had lent her and shook her horrific neon hair free.

'Oh, my darling!' he exclaimed sympathetically. Then, to Alex, 'We definitely start with the hair.' He bustled over and looped his arm through hers.

She threw a backward glance at Alex as Marlon propelled her from the room. He was settling into the lounge area with its leather sofas and complimentary wi-fi. As she watched he gave her a supportive grin and a wink. Her heart gave a warm and fuzzy little leap in return. He was impossibly gorgeous, and now he'd turned out to be less self-centred than she'd given him credit for. As he opened his laptop she looked away and caught a glimpse of herself in one of the mirrors. She grimaced. That had to have been a sympathy wink. The man dated the likes of Viveca Holt. He wasn't about to be making eyes at Ronald McDonald.

Marlon patted her hand comfortingly.

'Don't worry, sweetie,' he said. 'I like a challenge.'

If that was intended to make her feel better it failed miserably.

Ushered into a swivel chair in the hair salon and swathed in a protective gown, she was assigned a hairstylist who was intimidatingly young and trendy but who turned out also to be very sweet.

'I did a season on that reality talent show,' she confided reassuringly. 'Transforming contestants for the live per-formances. It takes more than a dodgy dye-job to faze me.'

A couple of hours and a make-up lesson later and Jen couldn't believe the girl in the mirror was her. Her new hair colour was gorgeous, with multi-layered tones of tof-fee and gold, and long layers made it swingy and glossy. The make-up was subtle—a bit of mascara, bronzer and pink-toned lippy. She could blend in easily with the girls at La Brasserie. Excitement bubbled in her stomach. After everything that had gone wrong, she finally felt as if she might be able to pull the article off, after all.

Marlon reappeared as she stood up and took off the gown.

'You look *fabulous*, darling!' he exclaimed delightedly, but then, as she glanced up to smile at him, he caught sight of the High Street jeans and old T-shirt combo she was wearing underneath and pulled a face. 'Shame about the ghastly clothes. Let's go and look through this stuff you've bought.' He led the way through another door. 'Don't you just love the internet?'

Her heart sank as she followed him into a dressing room with glossy black floor tiles and a three-hundred-and-sixty-degree range of brightly lit mirrors. She'd be able to view her bony hips and flat chest from every angle. Terrific.

He ushered her behind a screen.

Alex flipped idly through his e-mails and ordered another coffee from the starstruck junior. Jen had been gone a good couple of hours now. Enough time for him to finish making notes on a new and exciting script idea which made him itch more than ever to get back to work. Jen was fast becoming the only thing taking his mind off it, and he wondered if there were any other ways he could help her—other contacts he could enlist to help her succeed with her project. Living with her was anything but dull. He never knew what she might throw at him next. He realised with a flash of uneasiness that he was beginning to get off on that unpredictability.

He glanced through an e-mail from his PR company which recommended that he attend a charity ball this week, despite the fact he thought it would be media suicide. The charity funded grants for underprivileged youngsters wanting to build a career in film and Alex was a patron. Surely with the words 'casting couch' hanging over his head it wouldn't take much for a savvy journalist to come up with some sordid story about his association with them.

The PR company didn't see it that way. Reverse psychology, apparently. To be seen at the ball would show he had nothing to hide, that the stories about him and Viveca were groundless tabloid pap when they actually weren't.

It struck him with sudden amusement that his desire to party seemed to be disappearing. Since his life after Susan had been rebuilt as one long social event that was pretty damn unheard of for him. After failing so miserably at family life he'd gone for the opposite end of the spectrum, enjoying his situation to the full with no responsibilities to hold him back.

Worryingly, staying in was beginning to be more attractive than going out.

Once you realised his bonkers exterior was actually total perfectionism, Marlon turned out to be hilarious. And he was clearly harbouring a huge crush on Alex. He was devoted to him.

'He's never done this before.'

Standing in the middle of the circle of mirrors in flesh-coloured underwear, Jen was being treated to a view of her bony straight-up-and-down body that she could most definitely have done without.

'Done what?' she asked.

Marlon glanced up from the rail of clothes. She could see her own purchases in there among other stuff. He must have unpacked them while her hair was being fixed.

'Brought in a waif and stray.' He handed her the catsuit she'd bought with nightclubbing in mind. 'Put this on.'

She began to step into it, hackles rising.

'In fact, he's never brought in anyone on a one-to-one basis like this. We go to *him*, usually. Film sets. Awards ceremonies. He doesn't come to us.'

'I am not a waif or a stray,' she said, trying to look dignified with one leg in and one leg out of the catsuit. 'We have a working arrangement.'

He raised sceptical eyebrows at her over the rim of his statement glasses.

'He's helping me with an article,' she said. 'I'm a writer.' Oh, it filled her with joy to be able to say that to someone. 'He's using his contacts, one professional to another.'

'Sweetie, this is the first time he's ever had me style someone who isn't on his payroll. So you tell me what that means. And you're staying with him?' His voice rose with a hint of awe. 'People would *kill*! You've got closer than the rest of the population in the last five years. Not for the want of trying.'

He winked at her and she shook her head at him.

'You don't understand. We're not *together* at all.'

'Not yet, maybe.'

She didn't tell him she had Alex over a barrel with the threat of a front page tell-all. It was just so delicious to be thought alluring enough for it even to be *plausible* that Alex might be interested in someone like her. She opened her mouth to remind Marlon that Alex had seen her at her worst with her neon hair, but he cut her off with his own horrified squawk.

'Oh, my life! What blind, tasteless person chose *that*?'

Her intended pirouette in front of the scary mirrors in the brightly printed catsuit turned at the last moment into a damp squib of a wiggle. It *was* a designer label, wasn't it? Hadn't it cost practically a week's wages?

'It cost me two hundred pounds,' she said pointedly. 'Second-hand.'

'Sweetie, you were screwed,' he said to her reflection. 'Lesson one: bling does not equal class, girlfriend. Just because you spent a fortune on it, does not mean it will look good.'

He spent the next twenty minutes ordering her in and out of clothes, mixing and matching, adding accessories.

'I can't believe I'm the first person he's introduced to you who isn't working for him,' she said, dragging the subject back to Alex the first chance she got. 'I mean, come on.' She gave him a wink. 'I've seen the papers. He's always dating.'

'Exactly,' Marlon mumbled, then removed the pin he was holding in his mouth to speak clearly. 'He *dates*. That's the important word. It never lasts. He's never really interested and it's usually a mutual benefit.'

'How do you mean?'

'Those women he sees—all the same type, usually up and coming. Maybe with a movie in the pipeline or a DVD release to publicise. Nothing like being seen on Alex's arm to get a bit of exposure, and he gets a no-strings date out of it. Genius.'

'So it's more of a publicity stunt than anything?'

Her heart felt suddenly floaty. Maybe his playboy image was just that—hype, the papers twisting things. Perhaps there *could* be more to his helping her out than the damn agreement between them. He didn't have to do any of this, after all. She would have been happy with a few nuggets of advice from him. Her stomach felt suddenly melty at the thought of his interest in her being more than just… well, a *contractual requirement*.

'Well, of course he beds them,' Marlon said with brutal matter-of-factness, making her floaty heart plummet as if he'd stuck it with a pin. 'I mean Viveca Holt. Exquisite. Of course he beds them—who wouldn't?'

'Of course!' she said, with a chummy laugh that wasn't quite convincing enough to hide the fact he'd stamped on her feelings. Stupid feelings that she shouldn't be having.

'That's all it is, though, darling,' he comforted her. 'Don't you fret. He hasn't shown any real interest in anyone since the nightmare with his ex-wife.'

'I am *not* fretting!' she snapped.

Marlon made a cynical face. *Whatever you say,* it said.

'Did you know Susan?' she asked.

He pressed his lips together in a hard line.

'The wife?' He pulled a face. 'I knew them both. I worked on his first film. I wasn't long qualified myself, then. She was very normal. Not famous. Miss Ordinary. They were at college together.'

So Susan was like her, then. Nothing like the film star conquests Alex was linked to now.

'He's always been very close to his family. Probably thought he had it all. Happy families, career booming. No wonder it hit him so hard when it all went pearshaped.'

He flicked through the rack of clothes and produced a silk shift dress, cornflower-blue.

'You need to cinch in that waist to give you an illusion of curves while making the most of those legs,' he said.

'Did it come as a surprise to you when they broke up? she asked, hungry for more information.

'I think it came as a surprise to everyone—including Alex. Imagine that. You build yourself up from nothing, just get to the point where you don't have to worry about money, and then your wife calls the whole thing off and takes half of everything. Can't have been easy.' He fiddled with the waistline of the dress, not looking at her. 'And of course he didn't have a pre-nup. He wasn't anyone at all when they married, so she really did take him to the cleaners.'

She let Marlon finish the outfit. So the press stories were true. Susan had really hit him where it hurt—in the wallet. No wonder Alex wasn't keen on promoting any of his conquests from overnight guest to a more permanent position.

Had he thought he could trust Susan because she knew

the real Alex? The one before he became a celebrity gold-mine? She could see now why he surrounded himself with superficial relationships.

She was too preoccupied to be shy about Marlon's no-feelings-spared advice. By the time he'd put together out-fits for casual wear, dinner, cocktails and lunches, she was desensitised to standing in her underwear and wasn't even cringing any more.

'I'll just get changed back and then I'll be on my way,' she said, when he announced that he'd finished.

'You will *not*!'

He grabbed her saggy-kneed old jeans out of her hand, balled them up and threw them in the nearest bin.

'There's no going back now,' he said. 'Wear the clothes. Think class, not chav. Get yourself in character and stay there.'

He took her proudly by the arm.

'Now, let's show Alex what he's missing.'

Alex glanced up as the door opened, heaving a sigh of re-lief. He hadn't banked on it taking this long. Clearly what-ever horrific process Marlon had had to put Jen through to restore normality was more complicated he'd expected.

It was a moment before he saw her because she was shuffling nervously about behind Marlon.

'Well, what do you think?' Marlon beamed smugly, stepping aside. 'Isn't she just stunning?' He waited, clearly ready to bask in anticipated praise.

It took a moment for Alex to reply because his tongue had momentarily stuck to the roof of his mouth. When he'd driven her here this morning, half-eaten toast in her hand, his own borrowed baseball hat jammed over her eyes, she'd been girl-next-door Jen, still hanging her head over the monstrous hair mistake, and in spite of himself he'd been beginning to like having around far too much. Somewhere in the last few hours, under Marlon's supervision, the double cream skin had become lightly sunkissed and the ghastly orange hair had morphed into soft golden tresses.

'Wow,' he said eventually, because he'd only just regained control of the hinge of his jaw. A one-syllable word was about the limit of his capability right now. The golden tan made her blue eyes stand out more than ever, and the blonde highlights and freckled nose with her skinny figure made her look like an off-duty model just back from a shoot in the Bahamas.

He suddenly wondered at what point he had thought it would be a good idea to let Marlon loose on Jen. After all, she was never going to look *less* attractive, was she? Focusing on getting her out of her latest scrape with the horror hair and, he had to admit, enjoying the madness of it all along the way, it hadn't occurred to him that he might be making the situation a whole lot worse. If he was getting off on just being around her when her hair looked like a fright wig, it stood to reason that a makeover was only going to make things a shedload more complicated. He could kick himself.

A blush rose in her cheeks, making her look prettier than ever, and she ran a hand self-consciously through her hair.

'Does it look OK?' she asked him. 'Come on—give me your opinion.'

There was an awkward smile on her face that told him she wasn't completely comfortable with this. His heart gave a soft flip. The dark slim jeans made her legs look longer than ever. The shirt looked classy and expensive. She bore little resemblance to the shorts-clad indignant young woman with the bed-hair he'd found in his apartment a few nights ago. His stomach knotted with tension.

OK didn't even start to cover it. The collar of his shirt felt strangely tight, and it suddenly seemed degrees hotter in there. The freezing air outside was suddenly attractive. He'd been cooped up way too long.

'Terrific,' he blurted out. 'Excellent job, Marlon, as ever. We must get together soon and catch up.' He stacked his papers on top of his laptop and got to his feet. 'I need to get back and make some calls.'

What he really needed was to get out of this situation *right now*. He ignored her puzzled expression and made for the front door of the studio, bandying about promises to meet Marlon for lunch soon. Unfortunately not looking at her didn't go any way at all to numbing his sharp awareness of her as she followed him out, her high heels sounding every step she took on the tiled floor.

CHAPTER SIX

It was fantastic to wake up and look in the mirror and actually quite like what she saw for a change. Makeovers were seriously underrated, Jen decided. A few blonde highlights and make-up tips and she felt as if she could conquer the world single-handedly.

As long as the world didn't include Alex.

She squashed the churning disappointment she still felt at his lack of enthusiasm yesterday. He'd made barely any comment about her transformation and had disappeared to his study the moment they'd got back from Marlon's studio. She was furious with herself for minding so much. What was she expecting? That Alex Hammond, who had the pick of the world's most beautiful women, would swoon at the sight of her in a pair of designer jeans?

Yesterday had been a turning point. She'd been building their friendship up in her mind when to him it was clearly no more than a distraction from his own problem situation. He'd been sticking to his side of the gag order, nothing more, and she had been a fool to read anything else into it. Well, she was truly back on task now. Being here was all about work, nothing more. She intended to live the rich life properly, really get into character, do her article justice and make the sale.

Wearing the new jeans and a casual fitted shirt, she made her way to the kitchen for toast.

He was there, looking at his laptop screen with a face like thunder. He glanced up as she breezed into the room and went to the fridge. She removed a pint of milk and went to switch the kettle on.

'Morning,' she said, without looking round. Flatmates, that was all they were. 'Coffee?'

Alex realised he was staring at her with his mouth open and snapped his gaze away.

'Please,' he said automatically, not caring one way or the other about coffee. Watching the lithe way she moved around the kitchen was making him wonder what it might feel like to have those long, long legs wrapped around him.

For the hundredth time since yesterday he wondered just who would end up getting the benefit of her transformation. Who would she be targeting on her next madcap trip out? The thought caused a burning sensation deep in his chest. She might look like a super-confident socialite, but underneath all that gloss she was a kid with big aspirations. He felt an irrational angry aversion to this whole project that was so damned important to her.

'Can't you just write your article based on research?' he said suddenly. 'You know—do a few interviews, surf the net a bit?'

She turned from the coffee to stare at him, a bemused expression on her face.

'Well, I could, if I wanted to be like every other writer out there,' she said. She ran a hand distractedly through the perfectly undone hair. 'The whole point is that I live the experiment. Doesn't matter whether or not the plan works. It's the process that provides the background for the article. It's meant to be light-hearted, remember?'

'You mean it doesn't make any difference whether or not you actually manage to score a date with a guy?'

'Not to my article, no. I could write about where I went wrong and why it didn't work. But it would be great if it did work, because it would give me more material to play with. Why are you suddenly so interested?'

That was a good question. Why the hell was the idea of her throwing herself at some rich Lothario bothering him so hideously? Staring at these four walls was obviously making him lose the plot. He needed to get outside, get some perspective.

He didn't answer. Instead he looked back down at his laptop and forced himself actually to digest the e-mail from his PR manager, which he'd read now three times without actually taking in.

'...stay home as much as possible. Do not allow yourself to be photographed, except at events expressly cleared by us first. Any outings that may bring you into contact with members of the press should be approved by a member of the team...'

He stared at the words, anger finally tipping over the edge. Enough was enough. Right now he didn't care how many people had a stake in this film's success. He just wanted to live his own life again.

He logged out and shut the laptop, glancing up at Jen as she handed him a mug of coffee.

'What are you doing today?' he asked on impulse.

She took a sip of her drink, shrugged.

'Getting out and about,' she said. 'Testing out my new look.'

With a supreme effort he managed to stop himself looking down at her legs again.

'I'm going stir crazy here,' he said. 'Want some company?'

She stared at him, mouth open in surprise.

'Aren't you meant to be under house arrest?'

He stood up.

'A couple of hours won't hurt. I need to get out of here.'

'What if you get recognised?'

He crossed the kitchen and put the coffee down on the counter next to her. She was looking up at him dubiously, as if they were at school and he'd suggested they play some prank on a teacher. There was something irresistibly unspoiled about her. Before he could stop himself he'd slipped an arm around her shoulders and given her a squeeze.

'Don't worry,' he said. 'I've got a few places up my sleeve. And, anyway, what are they going to do? Give me detention?'

'Kensington Gardens?' she said.

He'd brought her to the smaller entrance to the gardens on the Bayswater Road—a low-key gate in black wrought-iron that was less attractive to tourists. So he wasn't completely throwing caution to the wind, then, no matter how stir-crazy he claimed to be feeling. She'd returned his baseball cap and he was wearing it himself today. With that partially obscuring his face, and a jacket with turned-up collar, he didn't seem to be drawing any second glances from passers-by.

He glanced sideways at her.

'You sound surprised.'

'That's because I am. You don't strike me as the kind of person who likes the great outdoors.'

They began walking down one of the elegant tree-lined avenues. The air was crisp but there was a hazy glow of winter sunshine tempering it. The trees were completely bare, dusted icy white. Their breath puffed out in soft clouds.

'Well, that just goes to show how little you know me,' he said. 'Sometimes a bit of open space is just the thing.'

'This is lovely. I've never been before.'

'You should do the sights. You've missed out.'

They began walking again down the avenue of trees. Frost clung to the grass. It felt as if they were walking through a Christmas card.

'Except for the Science Museum,' she added.

'The Science Museum?'

'School trip.'

He grinned down at her.

'London can be a fantastic place for kids,' he said.

'I'll expect you to relocate back here, then, shall I? In a few years, maybe, when you meet the right film star?'

'Very funny.'

'I'm being serious.' She kept her face straight. 'I'll probably be a senior editor by then, maybe on one of those glossy celebrity mags.' She looked up at the sky dreamily. 'I could do a fantastic photo spread. *Alex Hammond and family at their London home.*'

He didn't smile.

'That's never going to happen.'

'I'm a gifted journalist, you know! And I'm aiming high. The cheek!'

He still only cracked a faint ghost of a smile.

'I don't mean your ambitions. I wouldn't put it past you to end up editing *Vogue*. I mean me.' He paused. 'I'm not family material.'

She'd obviously touched a nerve. Her curiosity flared.

'Everyone is family material. Some people just don't know it yet. You're not exactly over the hill.'

'Not me.'

'I thought you had a happy family background? You told me you were close to your parents.'

She deliberately didn't mention his wife.

'I did. I had a good childhood. Hardly any money, but a happy home. Parents who loved me, not to mention each other. Brother who was also a good friend. I'm a psychologist's nightmare—there's nothing they could pin on my upbringing.'

'Don't you want to replicate that, then?' She was genuinely puzzled. 'With your financial position, you could do an even better job than your parents.'

'Yeah, well, I used to think that, too. But look at my life—the public scrutiny, the constant demands. Hell, my own ambition. How does all of that fit with having a family? We were always there for each other. That's how I was brought up. That's why they weren't crazy about my big career ideas. We were encouraged to be happy with what we had. My parents put us and each other first.' He shook his head. 'I can't be a father *and* make films at the level I want to. Not if I don't want to do one or both of those things substandard.'

The sound of children playing grew louder as they neared a playground. She dug her hands in her pockets to warm her fingers.

'Coffee?' he asked as they approached a café. The play area was bathed in hazy sunshine, with tepees and a huge pirate boat climbing frame with kids hanging off it.

'Hot chocolate,' she countered. 'I'll buy.'

He watched her queue for drinks. The place was full of families enjoying the winter sunshine. A long-discarded desire of his own had resurfaced and he crushed it down again. Family life or work success? That same old dilemma. To have both just wasn't an option. He knew that.

His choice was long since made—Susan's betrayal had certainly hammered the last nail in the coffin of any desire for a wife and kids—and he never discussed it. So why the hell was he revisiting it now?

She returned with the drinks and they carried on walking. Her cheeks and the tip of her nose were pink from the cold, frost sparkled on her eyelashes, and he fixed his gaze straight ahead to avoid watching her slowly sip the hot chocolate. As if he needed any more attention drawn to that soft pink mouth.

'There are lots of ways to crack a nut, you know,' she said, wrapping both her hands around her cup. 'My father wasn't there at all and I never felt neglected. It doesn't have to be all or nothing.'

She only vaguely registered two women approaching on the opposite side of the path—until one of them did a sharp double-take as they passed.

'Excuse me?' the dark-haired woman called out.

Jen stopped and turned, was aware of Alex doing the same. The woman was staring at Alex intently.

'Alex Hammond? It *is* you, isn't it?' She elbowed her companion. 'I told you I was right!'

Jen sensed rather than felt Alex tense next to her and squashed her own irritation at the interruption. She had felt for the first time that she was seeing beyond the exterior he showed everyone else. His being recognised now was the last thing he needed. She acted on impulse.

'Hah! He wishes!' she said, loudly enough to talk over any admission Alex might be thinking about making. 'I wish, too, come to that. Wouldn't mind Alex Hammond's money.'

Both women looked uncertainly towards her. Jen crossed her arms and looked appraisingly at Alex. He stared back at her, eyebrows raised.

'Can't say you're the first to say it, though,' she added.

'Really?' The woman eyed Alex with a frown. 'It's a remarkable resemblance.'

'You think so?' Jen said. 'That Alex bloke is far better looking, in my opinion. Roland's eyes are too close together.' She gave Alex a friendly punch on the arm. He was looking at her as if she were completely insane. 'No offence, honey.'

The woman took a couple of steps back, clearly disappointed.

'I was going to get my photo taken with him, post it online. I'm a mad fan. I've got loads of press cuttings about him.'

She saw a look of horror cross Alex's face, could see the unspoken word in his eyes. *Stalker!*

'You can have your picture taken with Roland if you like,' Jen offered. 'Better be quick, though, we're pitching for the management contract on the toilet servicing for the park. On our way to do a quick survey.'

That seemed to do the trick. The women drifted away.

Alex looked down at her, a grin lifting the corner of his mouth.

'Roland?' He said. 'That's the name that springs to mind when you look at me?'

'I was trying to put you as far away from reality as possible,' she protested.

'And my eyes are too close together?'

He fixed them on her and her belly gave an excited little flip in response.

'Nobody's perfect,' she said.

As they began walking again Jen tucked her arm through his. He was sharply aware of it, of the closeness of her. She probably walked arm-in-arm like that with all her friends, but it didn't stop his body reading more into it. Heat zipped up his spine and simmered on his skin just at the touch of her.

'Maybe we should make a move before she realises that actually your eyes *aren't* too close together,' Jen said, glancing over her shoulder. The women seemed to be lingering, still in sight.

He felt an unexpected pang of regret at the thought of ending the outing. He hadn't realised how much he enjoyed her ability to make him laugh, to put a light-hearted spin on every situation. The deep heat in his abdomen warned him that friendship was not the limit of his wanting and he crushed it. He wasn't about to lose control of his feelings just because she happened to make him smile.

'Let's find somewhere and grab something to eat. I know just the place,' he said.

On their way back, just a few turnings away from the apartment, was a small restaurant, smart but relaxed, with dark wood tables and a select menu. Coloured fairy lights were strung around the walls. The sky had darkened as they left the park and a thin veil of icy rain now coated the windows. Jen didn't mind. It felt intimate and cosy. They sat at a corner table and ordered steaks with caramelised onions, thin-cut crispy fries and hot coffee.

'You're not worried about being mobbed? I'd have thought you'd want to go home, not go to another public place,' she said as soon as the waiter had brought their food.

He sliced into his steak.

'I've yet to be mobbed in here,' he said. 'It's off the beaten track so it doesn't get touristy. Plus it's nearly two o'clock. The lunchtime rush is over.'

There were only two other tables occupied besides

theirs. No one gave them a second glance. She forked up some fries.

'So your father left when you were small?' he asked.

Jen felt the age-old defiance kick in. *Do not feel sorry for me.* 'Before I was born,' she corrected, and flashed back an I'm-not-bothered smile.

'That can't have been easy.'

She shrugged.

'You're assuming that he would have been someone worth knowing.'

'You don't know who he is?'

'Oh, I know,' she said, attacking her steak and slicing it into minuscule pieces. 'I just don't care.'

He looked questioningly at her and she put her knife and fork down, sat back for a moment, knowing she should just kill the conversation right there and then. She didn't have to tell him anything about her background. She found she wanted to. Maybe just a little.

'I was the result of a relationship my mother had with him,' she said. 'Well, I say relationship. It was a few nights, nothing more. He was her boss. He was married.'

She looked down at her meal, pushed the steak around a little with her fork, remembering.

'When she found she was expecting me, you can imagine it went down like a rat sandwich.' She grinned up at him ruefully but he only looked at her. 'As far as he was concerned he already had a family and a career. He didn't want to complicate any of that. My mother refused to have a termination so he dealt with it his way. Withdrew from her completely, never acknowledged me, went back to his comfortable life as if I never existed.'

'Your mum didn't spill the beans at all, then? To his family?'

She shook her head. 'She wanted to bring me up her-

self, without worrying about his intervention, so she never
stirred things up.'

She felt a pang of love as she thought of her mother.
How dignified she was. She'd accepted a one-off payment
and that was an end to it as far as she was concerned. But
Jen didn't want to go into that with Alex.

'And he's never tried to get in touch?'

She took a sip of her coffee and thought about the question for a moment, ran her mind back down the years when
she'd struggled with that lack of interest from her father.

'No,' she said, and considered how she felt about that.
'It probably bothered me most when I was school age.
Only because you don't want anything then that makes
you stand out from the crowd. And I wondered if I might
hear from him when I hit eighteen.'

'Bit of a milestone?'

She smiled bitterly.

'Also the age when you stop needing maintenance pay-
ments. I thought he might show his face. But nothing.
So when I hit twenty-one I didn't expect anything, and it
turned out I was right.'

'And if he turned up out of the blue now?'

'I couldn't be less interested.'

She forked up some steak and onions and carried on
eating her meal, not looking at him.

He watched her. All bravado. No wonder she was so
set on proving herself, so desperate for personal success,
to show herself as worthwhile. Despite the impression of
indifference she gave, it must hurt terribly that her father
had never even been intrigued enough about her to get in
touch. Not even once.

'Back to the grindstone after this, then?' he said, grop-
ing for matter-of-fact conversation, wanting to lighten
things up for her. And to distract himself from the com-

pelling need to ask more, dig deeper behind the façade to find the true Jen Brown.

She sighed. 'Yes. Shame, really. I could have spent all day in the park.'

'What's next up on your mad agenda, then? Now you're done with sorting out the clothes and hair?'

'Next I put it all into practice. Get myself into the same room as the target. I'm still on a budget, so I've thought up some ways of throwing myself into the path of eligible men without having to bankrupt myself on gallery tickets.'

Her voice became animated as she talked about her project. Alarm bells began ringing. What the hell was she cooking up now?

'What ways are you talking about?'

'There's a nightclub I thought I might try tonight. Christmas cocktails—that kind of thing. The younger royals hang out there sometimes. It's at the cutting edge of nightlife for the rich.'

He felt as if a bucket of sleet had been sloshed over him. The thought of her putting herself out there in some cattle market nightclub by herself, looking the way she did, filled him with cold horror. No man in his right mind would pass up the chance to spend time with her.

'You are *not* going out on your own to some nightclub,' he said before he could stop himself. 'I don't care if the Queen herself is a patron. You'll end up dead in a ditch somewhere.'

'There aren't any ditches that I'm aware of in Chelsea,' she said. Her excitement seemed to have slipped into obstinacy. 'And what's it to you where I go, anyway? I'd have thought you'd be pleased your part of the deal is finished. I've had the makeover, you've given me free rein to look through your wardrobe, and you've given me some pointers. I'm really grateful for all your input but I can manage on my own now. I've honed my skills and I'm confident I won't be throwing myself at any man worth less than a million.'

Alex was absolutely furious, and not inclined to explore too carefully where that level of feeling was coming from. He struggled to stay calm. He knew her well enough by now to be certain that if he forbade her to do something she'd press ahead with it all the harder. What he needed was something to divert her.

'Actually, I've got a better idea,' he said, thinking on his feet. 'And it would give you a lot more material for your article than you'd get hanging out at some nightclub.'

She looked at him suspiciously.

'What's that?'

'It's a Christmas ball tonight—for the Youth in Film charitable trust,' he said. 'I'm a patron. It's at a five-star hotel in Mayfair. There'll be a champagne reception, dinner, dancing. And an open charity auction. There'll be a big presence there from the film and media world. How about I get you a ticket there instead? You won't be able to move without falling over an eligible bachelor.'

And that way he could keep an eye on her from a distance. Make sure she was safe and not getting herself into any trouble. Surely that was the only reason he wanted her there?

Her eyes widened. 'Those events are way above my budget. They don't let just anyone in. In fact, it's probably not in keeping with the tone of my article—Miss Ordinary would never be able to afford to go.'

He rolled his eyes. Not this again.

'We've been through all this when I booked you in with Marlon. You need to start seeing past your principles if you're going to get the most top-quality material you can and write this thing. Who cares if you don't stick to the letter of the idea as long as you come up with an entertaining article that will blow their socks off? You keep telling me it's tongue-in-cheek. No Miss High Street from the back of beyond is really going to come to London armed with your article and intending to land a rich bloke. It's just meant to be entertainment.'

'I suppose so,' she said. Then she frowned suddenly.

'How come you didn't mention it before?' she said. 'I thought you were meant to be keeping out of the spotlight for a while? I know you've made a break for it today, but Kensington Gardens is hardly a paparazzi hangout.'

'I was in two minds about going, because it's a bit of a sensitive subject in light of the recent press stories about me. *Patron of charity that helps youngsters into film in casting couch scandal*—I can see the headlines now. But this way I'm showing I've got nothing to hide. Plus the charity relies on my profile, and it's a great cause. It would have made a massive difference to me when I was starting out if I'd had access to resources like that.'

She was practically jumping up and down with excitement now.

'Are you sure you can get me in? I can't believe this! I'll be able to get loads of background material.'

She tugged at his arm and leaned forward suddenly, gave him an impulsive quick peck on the cheek. Her skin was against his for a split second, but it was enough to send dizzying sparks sizzling from his skin to his abdomen via his spine. His heart began to race in his chest.

'Thank you,' she said. 'I'll give you a credit in the article.'

He leaned back deliberately in his chair, as if physically distancing himself would have the same effect on his mind.

'That won't be necessary.' He tried to keep himself on task. 'And there will be ground rules. I won't be able to spend the evening with you—you understand that, don't you? This isn't a date.'

She chuffed out laughter and he felt a little piqued. Was it really so outrageous a thought to her?

'Don't be daft,' she said. 'Last thing I need is *you* hanging around me, cramping my style.'

They finished their meal and began walking back to the apartment. Jen upped her pace considerably.

'Come on!' she called over her shoulder.

'What's the rush?' The crisp air caught in his throat after the warmth of the restaurant as he stared after her.

'Are you kidding me? It's going to be the poshest night of my life. I need to get back home and start getting ready.'

He checked his watch.

'But it's only mid-afternoon.'

'And your point?'

'The ball doesn't start until seven thirty. How much time do you need, for Pete's sake?'

She walked back to him impatiently, grabbed his hand and began walking backwards, pulling him along.

'You know what your problem is? You're just such a *man*. I have to look perfect.' Her voice rose excitedly. 'Ooooh, I get to wear my cocktail dress—yippee!'

He tried to stop himself zeroing in on the touch of her hand on his, on her bubbling enthusiasm. As he gave in and let her increase their pace he raised his other hand and snapped his fingers in front of her face.

'Pay attention. We'll have to arrive separately, leave separately, and no acknowledgment of each other beyond basic politeness. I can't afford to be linked with anyone else in the press—not now. The whole Viveca thing will be rehashed if I give them half a chance. So above all—

and this is really important—there cannot be a repeat of the art exhibition debacle. Whatever you do, you must *not* get drunk!'

CHAPTER SEVEN

Rule #5: Get thee to the right locations. Save as much of your budget as you can for some choice tickets to the right occasions. Charity dinners are the perfect choice—they are stuffed with the über-rich, desperate to part with their money for a good cause. All you need to do is watch and make your move...

EVENING wear. *Christmas party* evening wear. Glittery, goldy, silk, satin, velvet. A dream night out.

Make-up applied and hair finished, she held up the dress she'd chosen from an amateurish online photo which had passed Marlon's approval. A sumptuous full-length velvet gown in midnight-blue with spaghetti straps and a low draped décolletage. She put it on, zipped it up and walked down to the dressing room to stand in front of the mirror. It hung on her straight-up-and-down figure like a dishrag and the draped neckline looked like a huge wodge of spare flappy fabric. She took it off.

Thank goodness for shapewear. A girl's best friend.

She shrugged her way into a nude push-up bra and stuffed in the large-sized gel pads. Fortunately she wasn't planning on getting naked with anyone any time soon. They'd be in for a shock if she did. She stepped back into the dress and adjusted the neckline. Unbelievable. She could hardly recognise herself. She felt suddenly absurdly shy. Even though there was hardly an inch of her body that wasn't now fake in some way or other, in this dress she felt like a million dollars.

She glanced at the door, suddenly wanting Alex to see her looking her best for once, instead of her worst. Just to show him she wasn't only country bumpkin Jen. If she could impress him, with his string of supermodel girlfriends, she could impress anyone at the ball.

Before she could chicken out, she stepped into nude heels and made her way out of the room. Heart thumping in her ears, she checked the kitchen, then looked into the sitting room. The whole place was silent.

He'd already left.

Alex had spent what felt like hours mingling, being seen with the right people and saying the right things. Following PR advice, he deliberately hadn't avoided the press stalking the red carpet. He'd given a statement about the stellar work done by the foundation, and waited for the inevitable question about Viveca Holt. When it came he'd dashed off a carefully prepared reply.

'I'm grateful to Viveca for the outstanding work she's done on *The Audacity of Death*,' he'd said. 'Ours is a professional relationship. Anything more than that is pure speculation and, frankly, I think we should be focusing our attention this evening on the work of this charity instead of on idle gossip.'

He'd avoided follow-up questions, instead moving quickly through the glass revolving doors into the cool glossy cream of the hotel lobby, relieved that once inside the building the press were no longer a concern. Ushered to the silver and white elegant luxury of the ballroom, he'd taken a flute of champagne from an instantly present waiter and concentrated on socialising.

Half an hour in and not a foot wrong so far. He should be relaxing into the evening, but he couldn't shake the feeling of edginess that gnawed at his gut.

She was late. He should have insisted she use his driver instead of getting a cab.

He mentally kicked himself into touch. What the hell did it matter when she arrived? Or even *if* she did? This was him doing a favour for a friend, that was all. It meant no more than that.

'Looking for someone?'

Mark Dunn approached, hand outstretched, his wife trailing in his wake. Alex hadn't realised he was scanning the room so obviously. He pulled himself up mentally, forced himself to focus on his friend.

'Just seeing who's shown up,' he said, shaking his hand.

'Nice job with the press,' Mark said. 'You're getting to be something of an expert. Talking of which, how's the resident journalist?'

Late.

He shrugged. 'Since we got the gag order sorted, no problem at all,' he said. 'We barely see each other. She'll be moving out at the end of the month.'

He had no desire to discuss Jen with Mark or anyone else. She was already occupying far too much of his head. It suddenly occurred to him that she might have changed her mind at the last minute and gone to the nightclub, after all, what with her warped principles about not accepting help. The thought made him suddenly feel cold, and he turned to Mark to excuse himself, go outside and ring her on his mobile phone.

The words never made it past his lips. Instead the room seemed to freeze.

He found himself staring, mouth hanging open, over Mark's shoulder at the doorway, past the vibrant buzzing crowd. Because suddenly there she was.

He felt as if his eyes must be on stalks. When had Jen got curves like that? He was sure he would have noticed that cleavage if it had been there before. He could see growing confidence in her assured smile, in the way she walked tall, head held high. She was absolutely stunning.

He felt a thin sheen of sweat break out on his forehead and ran a finger around his suddenly tight collar. Moisture leeched from his mouth and he cut his eyes away in a hurry.

Oh, he was in so much trouble here.

He should have acted on that initial attraction the first night he'd met her. Seduced her into a quick fling, a few nights of fun—done and dusted. That was the root cause of all this. She'd have been out of his system by now, gone the way of all the others, Viveca Holt included. Instead he'd followed the stupid PR advice and kept his distance. He'd let himself get to know her, and in the process it seemed she'd somehow got under his skin, inside his mind. And he had no idea how to stop her.

Jen was one of a table of ten, and found herself included from the outset in buzzing, friendly conversation. The room was lit by huge chandeliers suspended from an ornate domed ceiling. Christmas flowers and swags of greenery studded with tiny pearly lights made everything festive. Circular tables were dressed in pristine white and silver, with sparkling crystal glasses and perfect silver cutlery. The waiting staff were smoothly efficient. A month ago this situation would have made her quake so badly with nerves that holding a knife and fork would have been a

challenge. Now she tucked into the starter of roasted scal-
lops with a celeriac purée without so much as a tremble.

She realised with a pang of something akin to guilt that
there was a part of her that could really come to like this
opulent lifestyle. Not just the beautiful food and elegant
surroundings here tonight, but the luxury of living in a
Chelsea apartment, too, and beautiful clothes. She'd spent
so long belittling this world in her mind, determined to believe it a façade filled with shallow people, that to admit
she was enjoying herself made her feel like a hypocrite.
She tried to focus on the fact that this was a means to an
end, about work not play. Enjoyment shouldn't come into it.

As the meal finished the auction began, hosted by a
well-known comedian who held the room effortlessly in
the palm of his hand. The man on her left knew exactly
what he wanted. She watched as he treated the just-for-fun
ambience with absolute seriousness.

'Not bidding?' he said as he won a weekend of hunting
and fishing on an exclusive estate somewhere in the North
for an unspeakable amount.

'I don't fish,' she said.

He grinned, raised his glass. 'Richard Moran,' he said.

Mid-thirties, with the most inscrutable dark eyes she'd
ever seen made even more striking by their contrast with
his fair hair. He was good-looking, she decided, in a men-
acing kind of a way.

He held out his hand.

She smiled and shook it.

'Genevieve Hendon,' she said. It actually helped, having
a false name. It was calming somehow. Jen Brown didn't
look like this—didn't come alone to places like these.

'On your own?' he asked.

'I am,' she said. 'I was meant to be here with a friend,

but something came up at the last minute. I couldn't bear to miss it so I came alone. How about you?'

She wanted to get as much background on him as she could in the shortest possible time. No point wasting her energy getting to know him if he wasn't eligible, after all.

He inclined his head.

'I came alone, yes, but I know a lot of people here. This is my field.'

She smiled, pouring as much interest into her tone as she could.

'Would I know any of your work?'

He gave her his full attention. 'Possibly,' he said. 'Have you heard of the *Faith* trilogy?'

Her heart began to pick up speed. The only way someone could avoid hearing of the *Faith* trilogy would be if they lived in a cave. Not award-winning arty stuff, by any means, but a total crowd-pleaser of a swashbuckling adventure franchise. It had broken box office records. She ran through her mental checklist.

Good-looking? Yes, despite the slightly unnerving eyes.

Rich? Definitely, definitely, definitely.

Eligible? Still to be discovered.

'What do you do?' he asked her. 'Are you in the industry?'

She laughed lightly.

'Nothing that exciting, I'm afraid. I'm building up to launching my own bespoke jewellery business.'

Marlon had helped her come up with that occupation. Something creative that might fit in with a wealthy background and didn't have her sitting on her backside living off her trust fund.

The bidding restarted. This time on VIP tickets to a sell-out Christmas race meeting. There was a buzz of excitement in the room.

'Excuse me one second,' he said, standing up. 'Someone I must speak to.'

She took the opportunity to scan the room. The women's outfits were nothing short of stunning, in every jewel colour she could think of and in the richest of fabrics—velvet, silk, lace. The men looked pristine in black tie. Way towards the front of the room at another table she was able to pick out Alex Hammond. She thought him the most handsome man in the room. Her heart turned over softly, making her catch her breath. No doubt along with every other woman in the room.

To her surprise his eyes seemed to be fixed on hers. She'd been expecting him to avoid her like the plague after the pre-ball pep talk he'd given her on the importance of keeping her distance. And now, bizarrely, he appeared to wave at her.

Surreptitiously she took a glance behind her—in case Viveca Holt was at the next table or something. Because surely he wouldn't be blowing his cover, not to mention hers, by openly greeting her like that. Nope, he was definitely waving at *her*. For Pete's sake. She gave him a smile that was more of a grimace and inclined her head as slightly as she could, hoping that would be enough of an acknowledgement to stop him.

Apparently it wasn't, because he raised a hand again. She looked away, heat rising in her face. Maybe he'd decided keeping his distance wasn't so important to him, after all. Her heart rate picked up at the thought. The idea that he might actually be interested in her filled her belly with butterflies and she took a deep calming breath. Tonight was about gathering material, not about swooning like some stupid teenager over Alex.

She would acknowledge him now and then stick to the original plan.

Raising a hand, she waved back to him in what she hoped was a coolly discreet fashion.

'Table sixteen. Thank you very much, miss. The total now stands at one thousand pounds exactly.'

The butterflies in her belly turned into concrete. A blinding spotlight pooled over her, making her blink like an owl. The eyes of the nine other guests at her table swivelled towards her, and she was favoured with approving smiles and claps as she realised what had happened.

She'd just bid a thousand pounds she didn't have on a trip to the races.

The room felt suddenly boiling. He hadn't been waving at her at all. He'd been bidding on the damn auction.

'Any advances on one thousand pounds?' the compère said.

She searched desperately for Alex across the room, but the spotlight made it impossible for her to pick him out. *Please let him bid. Please, please, please.*

Silence apart from background conversation.

She felt perspiration break out on her forehead. Much more of this and her make-up would begin to slide off.

'One thousand, one hundred with the gentleman at the bar...'

The spotlight slipped away as quickly as it had arrived and she felt suddenly as if she could breathe again. She took a calming swig from her wine glass, despite the fact she was determinedly pacing herself. The bidding carried on and she made a conscious effort not to move another muscle while the auction was going on. Crisis averted— no thanks to Alex. Wait until she got her hands on him.

Returning to the table in time for coffee, Richard Moran talked about himself animatedly. Within minutes she'd established he was single. That was all the boxes ticked. The perfect target. Plus he was openly flirting with her.

The problem was she felt anything but enthusiastic about spending the evening with him. As she tried to work out why there was a nagging feeling of disappointment deep inside her, she found her eyes straying far too often to the table across the room where Alex was talking seriously to the stunningly beautiful woman seated on his right.

As soon as the auction had closed the band began a classy jazz set, and Alex watched as Richard Moran led Jen by the hand to the dance floor. He took her in his arms, his hand pressed against the small of her back.

There was no point even bothering to deny it any more. The seething heat deep in his gut was too strong. He was horribly, angrily jealous. Of all the men she could have ended up with it had to be *him*. A business rival he truly disliked. He insisted to himself that this was about Richard Moran, not about Jen, and refused to acknowledge the needling thought that he'd be feeling like this about any man in the room she spoke to.

Good intentions or not, he'd had enough. He had to intervene before she went too far. She wasn't the worldly-wise socialite she was pretending to be. And that meant she was out of her depth without even knowing it. As Moran led Jen to the edge of the dance floor he crossed the room towards them and waited to pick his moment.

'Another drink?' he heard Moran ask.

'Just mineral water, please,' Jen said.

At least she was pacing herself with the alcohol. With any luck she'd keep her wits about her and take on board what he was about to say.

As soon as she was left standing alone by one of the huge marble pillars Alex approached, took her hand and led her firmly back onto the dance floor. The band played a slow number, and the dance floor slowly filled up. He steeled himself against the heat that climbed through his body as he pulled her against him, slid a hand around her tiny waist. The soft velvet of the dress clung to every contour of her body, giving an intoxicating hint of how it might feel to hold her naked against him. The sweet scent of her hair made his mind spin. She looked up at him in surprise, the soft pink mouth close enough for him to kiss her with just a short movement of his head.

With a stupendous effort he focused on the task at hand and hissed at her in an urgent whisper. 'What the hell are you doing?'

Her brows knitted. 'I might ask you the same thing. Thanks to you I nearly bought a trip to a race meeting when I've got zero cash and I loathe horses. I thought you were waving at me. And I thought we were meant to be avoiding each other at all costs.'

'We are,' he said. 'I just can't stand by and watch you spend the evening with Richard Moran without warning you about him.'

She pulled away a little to look up into his face, a puzzled expression in her eyes.

'Why would you want to warn me about him? It's going brilliantly. He's the perfect target. Did you see how high he went with the bidding for that vile hunting holiday? He's obviously completely minted, he's here on his own and he isn't a total nightmare to look at. In my book that ticks pretty much all the boxes.'

'It doesn't matter if he gives millions to charity. He can't be trusted. He'll do anything to get what he wants.'

She came to a standstill, forcing him to do the same. They stood motionless, surrounded by dancing couples. Her expression was fierce.

'He's in film production, isn't he? Just like you.' She held up a hand and cut her eyes away from his. 'Look, I'm really grateful for all the help you've given me, but that doesn't give you some kind of creative veto over my work. I can take it from here by myself, thank you very much. He's perfect, and I'm not backing off just because he happens to be some work rival of yours.'

If only the reason was that simple.

'That has nothing to do with it. I'm looking out for you. He's not a nice guy.'

She rolled her eyes. 'What do you mean?'

'Let's just say he's involved in some pretty shady stuff. If he gets a sniff that you're chatting him up under false pretences it won't be pretty. Don't kid yourself that he'd see the funny side of your damn article. He could ruin your whole career with one phone call if he wanted to. You're not used to mixing with these people. You haven't a clue what you might be dealing with.'

He could see immediately that he'd said the wrong thing. Her eyes widened in anger.

'Don't you *dare* patronise me! Just because I'm not swimming in cash doesn't mean I'm not up to dealing with people who are. You make it sound like I'm some social moron. I thought you were different, but I was wrong. You're just like the rest of them here—certain that you're better than everyone else.'

'I didn't mean it like that,' he said. Where on earth did this paranoia of hers about not fitting in come from?

'I can handle Richard Moran,' she snapped. 'He's never going to know who I really am. It's one evening. That's all. I'm hardly likely to get much further than small talk, but I am going to end up with *tons* of information for my article. So if you could make yourself scarce that would be great.'

She raised her eyebrows and kept them there until he took a step back, and then she turned to walk back across the room to where Richard Moran waited for her like a predator, with a drink in each hand. His blood felt as if it might hit boiling point at any moment. He pushed his way through twirling couples to the other side of the room and was quickly surrounded by people wanting to discuss the evening, the charity, any forthcoming award nominations. He tried to focus outwardly on his own purpose for the evening—being seen to be on the straight and narrow, championing a good cause.

It felt to him as if Jen was lit up by a huge spotlight that kept everyone else in the room in shadow. What was happening to him? He barely remembered his girlfriends' names usually, and now he seemed to be aware of every tiny detail about *her*. The gorgeous curve of her neck softened by the tumbling golden curls, the stunning slender figure hugged in all the right places by the rich velvet of the dress. He wanted to slide his arms around her again and feel her body against his, responding to his every movement.

He forced himself to get a grip. He was meant to be keeping his nose clean, living a quiet life, focusing as he always did on work. She had brought nothing but trouble since the day they'd met. He'd long since given everything to his career, and he damn well wasn't going to let that be compromised again by a woman.

As Jen took to the dance floor again, back in the arms of Moran, Alex forced himself to look anywhere but at them.

Inside he fought the impulse to cross the room and tear Richard Moran's head from his shoulders.

CHAPTER EIGHT

Rule #6: Rich men can always be found near boats, horses and ski slopes. Get yourself to any of these locations and make sure you know what you're talking about.

ALEX unlocked the door to the apartment and tried to engage his tired brain, which currently felt as if it was packed in cotton wool. A reversion to type had seemed like a great idea earlier, as he'd watched Richard Moran twirling Jen expertly around the dance floor. The ideal way to get back some perspective—which he'd clearly lost if he'd begun to obsess like this about a woman.

It was the stress of his recent press exposure. Had to be. Pressure from all sides to get some positive publicity had taken its toll. His enforced abstention from the opposite sex had made him become preoccupied by the nearest woman. One who couldn't be more unsuitable if she tried. She might look delectable, but that didn't compensate for the fact she was a walking disaster area, always causing chaos, always in some kind of scrape.

At first the decision to let her get on with it had seemed a liberating one. Let her spend the evening with that idiot Moran. It didn't mean he had to watch her do it. He'd made his excuses at the ball and gone on to a club. Maybe exactly what he needed was to get back to normal, and have a full-on meaningless fling, and damn the consequences.

The problem was none of the women at the ball or the club had held the remotest speck of interest for him. Try as he might, there was only one woman he wanted to spend time with. He could deny it all he wanted. Apparently it wasn't going to go away.

He headed to the kitchen to make some coffee. He would go to the study, work for a couple of hours. Sleep was beyond him now. The anger that had seethed all evening as he watched Jen flirt with Richard Moran was still simmering just below the surface. And adding to it was hatred of these insane feelings for her that were apparently beyond his control.

'Richard Moran was nothing short of the perfect gentleman,' Jen said airily the moment Alex stepped into the kitchen. For some reason the satisfaction she'd expected to get from saying that to him didn't live up to the anticipation.

'You waited up for me just so you could say *I told you so*?'

Hmm. She supposed it did really boil down to that. Not that she was going to tell him.

He threw his keys on the counter, filled a glass with water from the fridge and immediately downed half of it. *Hah!* Obviously dehydrated. She'd been looking forward to being the sober one with the moral high ground for a change. Surely sloping in at one-thirty a.m. automatically meant a few drinks too many?

Unfortunately not. The green eyes were absolutely sharp and lucid. Worse, the intense way he was looking at her over the rim of the glass was making her stomach feel melty and her pulse pick up speed.

'I am *not* waiting up for you,' she snapped. 'I've got a ton of notes to write up on the evening. Best to do it while it's still fresh.' She waved a hand at the laptop and the notes covering the counter in front of her. 'I just didn't realise it was so late.'

She narrowed her eyes at him suddenly.

'Anyway, how do you know I didn't just get in myself? For all you know I could have been whisked off to dance the night away.'

'Er…you're wearing pyjamas.' He raised an eyebrow and nodded down at her open dressing gown and shorts and vest combo.

Damn. She'd forgotten about that. Understandable, considering how annoyed she was with him. His implication that she was out of her social depth with men like Richard Moran had really rankled. She knew she was overreacting, but she couldn't seem to help herself. It had needled her more and more as the evening had progressed.

When Richard's driver had dropped her home at half past eleven her first thought had been to sweep inside and run through the huge success of the evening with Alex. Prove him wrong. OK, so Richard had a bit of a propensity to ogle her fake cleavage, but she could put up with that because he also loved the sound of his own voice and had given her loads of material to write about. She'd seen no sign of the scary villain Alex had made him out to be.

Having to wait two hours to prove him wrong had somehow made her irritation spread into a massive annoyance with herself for wondering where he was, what he was doing and, worst of all, who he was doing it with. Because she really shouldn't give a damn about any of those things.

No way was she letting on that she'd been sitting here that long. Not when he was obviously more than happy to have got some distance between them. He'd taken her at her word and disengaged himself totally from her and her project. She hadn't even seen him again after he'd warned her off Richard.

So much for his concern for her safety and wellbeing. He was so concerned that the moment their conversation was over he'd disappeared for the rest of the night. No doubt living it up—probably with the exquisite blonde from his table at the ball.

He pulled a stool up next to hers and looked at the mess of papers and the open laptop in front of them. She was acutely aware of how close he was. Well within touching distance. She could breathe in the scent of his aftershave and she felt a dangerous flutter deep in her stomach.

'Aren't you going to ask me how I got on?' she asked.

He took another sip of water.

'Nope.'

'Well, I'll tell you,' she said, ignoring the *here-we-go* roll of his eyes. 'Richard told me all about his home in Hollywood, and his ranch in Montana. Not to mention his mansion in the Cotswolds. He has a yacht, he dabbles in horse racing and he's fed up with airhead women who aren't up to the challenge of stimulating conversation.'

Alex rubbed his eyes with a thumb and forefinger.

'Let me guess—that's where you come in, is it?'

'Absolutely,' she said triumphantly. 'Once you've found out a man's background and interests, you're well on the way to snaring him. It stands to reason. He barely left me alone for five minutes. He was gobsmacked by how much we have in common. Well, how much he *thinks* we have in common.'

He gave a bitter laugh.

'I just bet he was.'

She threw her hands up in exasperation.

'I don't understand this. Why can't you be pleased for

me? I thought we were friends. You've helped me do all this groundwork for my article—getting Marlon involved, helping me prepare. And now, when I start to have some success, when I actually manage to engage a man's interest, you tell me I'm not up to the challenge of dealing with him. Your implication that I'm some hopeless case who can't hold her own in rich company was *so* offensive.'

Elbows on the counter, he ran both hands through his hair.

'That is *not* what I was saying!'

She could tell by the strangled tone of his voice that he was struggling to maintain control.

'I was trying to do you a favour, look out for you, and for some reason—God only knows what—you've chosen to see it as criticism of *you*. You've got this huge chip on your shoulder about fitting into what, let me tell you, is nothing but a false world full of shallow people. Why the hell do you want so much to be a part of *that*? You saw it tonight. It's all about getting along with the right people, keeping them sweet, greasing palms. You think I actually *like* half those people I was with tonight?'

She felt oddly naked, as if he could suddenly see inside her, pick out her insecurities. She dropped her eyes from his as if they were giving her away, fiddled with the papers on the counter.

'It's not that I want to be a part of it,' she said, and in her tired and overemotional state she added before she could check herself, 'It's that I could have been. If my life had panned out differently.'

He frowned. 'You're not making any sense.'

She almost told him then. Who her father was. The way he'd paid off her mother instead of accepting Jen as his child before melting back into his opulent life with his wife and privileged legitimate children. There was so much bitterness there that she didn't know how to start—wasn't sure she wanted to. She bolted back to her comfort zone, where the whole situation was about work and nothing else.

'Forget it,' she said. 'It doesn't matter. What matters is my work. Getting this article finished and sold. And, like it or not, Richard Moran has given me better material than I could have hoped for.'

He clenched his hands, glanced up at the ceiling.

'OK, I apologise! Is that what you want to hear? I'm sorry if I belittled your achievement. That wasn't my intention.'

'What *was* your intention, then?' she snapped.

She sought the answer in his green eyes, waited for him to speak. And in the depths of that moment he was suddenly on his feet, reaching for her, one hand sliding into her hair, cupping the side of her face, tilting her mouth to meet his, the other claiming her waist.

The attraction she'd tried so hard to crush since she'd lain beneath him that first night flooded back. Sparks tingled on her skin at his touch, zinged down her spine, and heat seemed to pool at the top of her legs. If it hadn't been for the stool she might well have folded like jelly onto the floor.

The space between them was hers for the taking, and before she had time to think take it she did. She was on her feet, too, palms sliding up the taut muscle of his chest to meet around his neck, fingers sinking into his hair. His hand curled around her waist in an urgent caress as he moved backwards again to the stool, hooked one foot around her and pulled her greedily into the gap between his legs. He moulded her body hard against his and she moved her hips against him in response. She could feel the effect she was having on him. He uttered a low guttural moan. She felt his hand slip beneath her pyjama vest, sliding across her skin and making her jump and writhe with desire. The other hand tangled in her hair, tilting her head to the perfect angle as he parted her lips hungrily with his tongue.

Only now she'd responded to him did he take full control. And that was what finally made common sense kick back into her spinning mind.

Better late than never.

Equal responsibility. That was how he wanted it. No comeback. That was how he played it with women, wasn't it?

He was obviously missing his social life. He'd gone out partying after the charity dinner, had stuck to his stupid single-in-public rule. Was that because he knew he had his own manufactured socialite back at home, gag order in place, ready to go? She'd turned herself into his kind of arm candy, signed away her right to tell anyone what happened between them and suddenly—what a coincidence—she was fair game.

She disengaged herself from him, took a good couple of paces backwards. He didn't protest, didn't try to move towards her. He simply stayed where he was on the stool, watching her. He rubbed his lips with his fingers as if savouring the taste of her.

She tried to take control of her racing heart.

'Got your gag order in place so now it's all systems go?' she said, trying not to pant.

His eyes held hers, widening slightly in surprise.

'The gag order has nothing to do with this,' he said.

'Really? Your models and actresses are off the menu, aren't they? I've been living under your roof these past couple of weeks and the only time you noticed the way I looked was when my hair turned into a fright wig. But add a load of gloss and fake extras...the nails...the breasts...

and get yourself a gag order—suddenly I'm up for grabs. Now that I look like a clone of one of your conquests.'

He smiled at her, the lopsided grin melting her very bones.

'I can see where you might get that idea from, but you're wrong,' he said. 'The agreement has nothing to do with this. I wanted to kiss you. You gave as good as you got. Don't try and hide that by criticising my motives. Why kiss me back if you didn't want to?'

She ignored him—along with the frantic pounding of her blood and the vague sense that she might be overreacting.

'I know the kind of man you are. Your life is an open newspaper. The women you step out with are the kind who spend a fortune on their appearance and always look perfect. It's obvious that's what does it for you these days.'

'So you think you only look good to me now you've spent hours getting your hair and nails and goodness-knows-what-else done?'

He got down from the stool, closed the gap between them so that she needed to look up to watch his face. She was hotly aware of his muscled body inches from hers, of every cell in her body wanting to take that one pace back into his arms.

She stood her ground and looked at him boldly. 'In a word, yes.'

He gazed right into her eyes as he spoke.

'You. Are. Gorgeous,' he said. 'In that dress tonight. In jeans and a T-shirt. And most of all in these hideous short pyjamas with your hair looking like you've spent the night screwing instead of sleeping. I really wish you weren't. The idea was for me to avoid women, play the single professional for a bit, and having to share my roof with you, and those legs, was *not* part of the plan.'

Her oversensitised body fought for control over her mind. She was furious with herself for responding to him and livid with the unfairness of it all. The strongest physical reaction she'd ever had to any guy and it had to be someone like him—someone who held all the cards.

'And you see this as more than a one-night stand, do you?' she asked. 'More than your usual casual fling? You want to step out with me in public? Or maybe introduce me to your parents? Are you looking beyond tomorrow morning for a change? Possibly the end of the week? Maybe New Year?'

He simply looked at her. And in his silence she realised how stupidly disappointed she was.

She was most definitely *not* going to have a fling with him. No matter how gorgeous he was. No matter how much her body wanted her to. She was in total control here. Let him realise he wasn't irresistible. Kick that arrogance into touch. So his kiss turned her legs to jelly? That didn't mean she had to betray the effects, give him the satisfaction.

His lips were inches from hers.

'It isn't going to happen,' she said softly, looking into his eyes. His warm breath mingled with hers. 'I don't do rich men, I don't do flings and I definitely don't do flings with rich men. Especially ones who manipulate their way through life with gag orders, contracts and cash. So why don't we stick to our own plans? I'll get my article finished and be out of your hair by Christmas. And you can get on with sorting out your reputation. If you've still got one.'

With enormous effort she took a step back from him, then put another pace between them, and another. His gaze didn't waver, meeting hers without a hitch until she cut her eyes away and left the room, slamming the door behind her. She knew just from the way her nerves were on edge that she'd be lucky to get any sleep tonight, but she didn't care. She was in control, not Alex, and that was the only thing that mattered.

Alex stared for a long moment at the closed kitchen door. She'd had to kick the doorstop away because she was so determined to have something to slam. If his head wasn't so mixed up he might have found that amusing.

Desire burned deep in his abdomen. He rubbed his fingers slowly over his mouth again. He could still taste her, still smell her. His senses were vibrantly alive. He couldn't remember the last time he'd felt so tuned in to a woman, and he was so damn sexually frustrated he felt like gnawing the granite worktop.

Kissing her hadn't been the plan. Of course it hadn't. He'd been fighting those mad feelings like crazy all evening. And suddenly those soft lips had been against his. He was shocked by the overpowering hunger that suffused every part of his body. Rational thought was driven away. The pent-up anger and jealousy he'd suppressed all evening as he watched her in someone else's arms boiled to the surface. His one desire at that moment was to kiss and kiss and kiss her again, and ride that delicious wave as far as he could.

He stood up and made coffee. The familiar motions of filling the mug, adding milk, calmed him, brought a more solid reality back.

It gnawed at him that she'd painted him as some kind of predator, out to take advantage of her. And it annoyed him even more that he cared so much what she thought. He'd had a lucky escape. He was tired, wasn't thinking straight. She might look like Miss Chelsea now, but underneath she was country village girl through and through.

Miss Ordinary. Like Susan. Do-not-touch-with-bargepole. Rationality clicked coldly back in.

He drained his coffee and threw the dregs down the sink. As he made his way to his bedroom he felt the momentary lapse in control disappear. She'd done him a favour, backing off like that. The next time he saw her he'd make sure he kept a safe distance. Physically and mentally. And surely now her work would be done she'd be moving out. That was a good thing.

Yet sleep was still a very long time coming.

On edge through lack of sleep, Jen was dressed by seven, making coffee and breaking eggs into a frying pan. She added milk and began to scramble them. Her head felt fuzzy and out of focus.

Alex came into the kitchen and her heart skipped a beat. Despite her mental determination to put distance between them her body was apparently refusing to stand down. Even when obviously tired he still looked gorgeous. He poured his own coffee. The tension in the room was palpable.

'Hi,' she said uncertainly.

He barely glanced around.

'Morning.'

'I'm going to be working on a draft of my article today—the material I've got so far. I thought I'd set myself up in the den, if that's OK with you?'

There was a pause, as if he was considering whether to mention the elephant in the room.

'About last night…' he said.

She'd prepared for this. Somewhere in the long restless hours between leaving him in the kitchen and finally giving up on the prospect of sleep.

'There was no last night.'

He looked vaguely amused. 'You can deny it as much as you like. I was there, too, remember?'

'I meant what I said. Let's just be professional. Concentrate on our own lives.'

'I couldn't agree more. But first, for the record, I did *not* take advantage of you, despite your determination to paint things that way. You kissed me back.'

'You made me.'

He laughed in disbelief. 'I'm sorry?'

'I said, you made me.' She had to admit, as arguments went, it wasn't her strongest.

'I've only known you a matter of days but I think I can say with confidence that I can't imagine anyone *making* you do something you didn't want to. Ever.'

Deep down there was the frustrating reality that he was right. She *had* kissed him back. But only after *he'd* instigated the intimacy. She rounded on him, determined to put an end to this once and for all.

'However you want to paint things, we both played a part,' she said. 'I don't see why this has to turn into a huge *atmosphere*. I just want to make it clear that last night was a blip. I'd never be interested in a one-night stand.' She tipped the eggs onto a plate. 'It's nothing personal.'

He gave a bitter laugh. 'One-night stand? Is that what you think it would be?'

'What do you expect me to think? You don't do relationships. You do work. You made it clear how you live your life. You want short-term flings with no comeback. That's fine by me, but I'm not about to be a one-hit wonder. Not for any man.'

Alex thought of Susan. The sweetness of their early relationship, the distance that had grown gradually between them as his work became more and more demanding in line with his success. And the end, when he'd realised he no longer knew her at all. If he ever had. The side of the story the press hadn't covered.

'Of course you're at such an advantage because you think you know all about me,' he said. 'Everything there is to know about my past. Because everything printed about me is, of course, always true.' His voice rose to an exasperated snap.

She didn't rise, kept her voice calm. 'Tell me what you're really like, then. What am I missing? Why shouldn't I believe everything I read about you?'

How the hell was he supposed to answer that? And, more to the point, why did he even want to? She had the weight of years of tabloid stories on her side, painting him as a playboy. He'd been linked to so many women. Some were just speculation, but plenty had been correct. Oh, yes, the papers had made much of the financial cost of his divorce. But there had been other costs, too—ones which didn't make such great column inches. He was so much more newsworthy as a bachelor playboy rather than a workaholic who dated superficially because he had no time to be a family man.

He gripped the edge of the granite counter, took a breath, and wondered where to start. Wondered whether to start at all.

The sound of the exterior intercom buzzing cut like a knife through the tension in the kitchen. For a moment both of them stuck to their rigid defensive posture. Jen looked at him expectantly for what she was no doubt certain would be a rubbish explanation. Then she threw her hands up and left the room for the front door.

He heard her speaking, heard the door open and shut, and then she re-entered the room. The only visible part of her was the long legs. The rest was obscured by a gigantic arrangement of red roses, holly berries and Christmas greenery. An explosion of red and green, vulgar in its hugeness. He felt his jaw drop.

She heaved the arrangement onto the kitchen table. He couldn't help noticing that her cheeks were flushed pink with excitement as she emerged from behind the flowers. She pulled out the card and flipped it open.

A sharp intake of breath gave away her delight. 'They're from Richard Moran!' she said.

Of course they were. Hadn't he known that the moment he saw them? The man had no style. The massive bouquet dominated the room. Moran had never been one to stick to the mantra of less is more.

Lack of subtlety didn't seem to make a poor impression on Jen. She looked at him, card held aloft, delighted excitement in her eyes.

'He's invited me to the racing!' she gasped. 'That VIP Christmas meeting I accidentally bid for. He must have thought I wanted to win it and couldn't afford to go higher!'

Alex felt a nauseating stab of jealous irritation that told him that, however hard he denied it, last night's kiss definitely meant more than he wanted it to. What a creep! He couldn't believe she was falling for this.

'You can't seriously be thinking about going? You just finished telling me how much fantastic material you've got. How much more do you need, for Pete's sake?'

She looked at him with an incredulous expression.

'Of course I'm going! Are you insane? I need to ride this out as far as it goes now. That's the whole point of the article. This is better than I could ever have hoped.'

'The longer you go on with this, the more likely it is he'll clock who you are. It might have been OK last night, with all those people, the dancing and the auction in the background, but if you spend the day at the races, just the

two of you, he's bound to ask you some awkward questions.'

'Your confidence in me is really heartening,' she said,
giving him a sarcastic grin.

'Your insistence on pushing ahead with the project is
very telling,' he snapped back angrily. 'Are you sure it's
really still about the article? Are you sure you're not getting carried away with the moment?'

The flush on her cheeks intensified and she cut her eyes
away from his.

'Don't be ridiculous! Nothing is more important to me
than nailing this article. Everything is riding on it. All my
savings are sunk into it, and my future career depends on
it. I don't care what it takes.'

'Don't you think you might be protesting a bit too much?
You don't care if you're taking a risk because you're so
busy swooning over your new fake life, being wined and
dined by a millionaire. So much for social experiments.'

He knew he'd touched a nerve. Fury took over her face.

'You have absolutely no idea what you're talking about.
I am here to work. Last night was about research for my
article—not cosying up to some rich guy, getting what I
could out of it. This whole thing is about making my own
success without the need for any of that.'

'You expect me to believe that?'

'I don't care if you believe it.'

'I've seen all this before, you know. Starting out
grounded, determined the lifestyle won't change you.
Then you have a taste of the high life, start to enjoy the
trappings. It's one slippery slope to letting the luxury take
over. You lose your grip on reality, on what was really important to you at the outset.'

He saw from the knit of her eyebrows, the sudden

shrewd gaze, that he had her full attention now. But her next question still floored him.

'Are you talking about yourself?' she said.

He wanted to kick himself for giving away so much, and cursed her insight.

'Not just about me,' he said shortly.

'You mean your marriage?'

He was done with this conversation. 'Yes, I mean my marriage. I won't bother to elaborate. I'm sure you already know all the details as you're so up to speed with the press coverage of me. And if you don't you can always research me on the internet.'

He left the room. Left her to the flowers. He didn't see her blush because she'd actually done that way back, on the first day she met him.

CHAPTER NINE

'LET me get this right. Alex Hammond snogged you and you've told him you're not interested?' Elsie's incredulity was immense. 'Have you lost your mind?'

'No, I haven't! And that's exactly the point. I'm in total control of the situation. Men like Alex Hammond do not go for women like me. Not for any good reason, anyway. He only took an interest because he's had to swear off women after all that stuff about Viveca Holt in the news. He can't get his hands on one of his usual conquests so he thought he'd have a punt at me. He'd probably cosy up to a gorilla right now if it had a makeover and signed a gag order.'

'Who cares what his reasons are? You passed up the chance of a fling with Alex Hammond!' Elsie spoke as if Jen had won the lottery and handed the ticket back.

'Yes! Exactly! All it would ever be is a *fling*. Because that's all he ever has.' Jen smoothed her hair back from her face, took a dignified breath, drew herself up to her full height. 'I'm better than that.'

Perhaps if she said that often enough, in lots of different ways, she might actually begin to feel as triumphant about her decision as she wanted to feel. Instead of this miserable dragging in her stomach as if the butterflies he'd evoked there last night had been doused in icy water. The idea that she might be different, more than a week-long fling, was something she refused to entertain. She'd bet all his girlfriends thought they'd be the ones to change him, and if Viveca Holt hadn't managed it Jen from the country wasn't likely to, was she?

She made a huge effort to squash everything out of her mind apart from her article. It was about time she got her mind back on task.

'Only problem is, now I need some background information on horse racing and I can't ask him. I'm having to rely on the internet and I feel like I'm floundering. I don't suppose you know anything?'

'Nope. Sorry.'

Impossible to distract, Elsie returned to the subject that mystified her. 'Was he a good kisser?'

Just the flashback that question prompted made Jen feel like melting into a puddle on the floor.

'I'm not going to answer that,' she said. 'I'm going now.'

She moved to press the disconnect button, but not before she managed to catch Elsie's parting comment.

'That means yes.'

Rule #7: Never fall at a millionaire's feet. Remember he has hundreds of women doing that. Remain cool, classy and in control at all times.

It turned out that the careful couple of glasses of champagne at the ball—just enough to make her feel confident and bubbly, not enough to turn her into loudmouthed ladette—combined with the twinkly subdued lighting, had given her a bit of a rose-tinted goggles effect when it came to Richard Moran.

Perching uncomfortably on one side of the leather back seat as his car purred smoothly towards the racetrack, it briefly occurred to Jen that Alex's warning her off him might also have pushed Richard up a few notches on the attractive scale. She'd been told many times, mainly by her mother, that there was a definite streak in her that didn't appreciate being told what to do.

In the cold light of day Richard was ogling her cleavage rather too much for comfort. Then again, the moss-green dress with its pretty floral print and empire line didn't need stuffing with chicken fillets to make it look half decent. Perhaps he was simply wondering where her curves had gone.

His incessant talking about himself and name-dropping was also beginning to grate on her, and his hands were getting a bit wandery, making her grateful to whoever had invented the maxi-dress that it banned access from ankle to neckline. She sat up stoically in the seat. She wanted so much to write a mind-blowingly brilliant article. One the editor of *Gossip!* magazine simply couldn't refuse. The consummate professional, that was her. She was prepared to do anything to pull that off.

She wriggled away as Richard's hand brushed her thigh.

Not quite anything.

Alex drained his fifth coffee and tried to apply his caffeine-buzzing mind to his work. Just his work. Everything else excluded. Doing that was meant to be second nature by now. Relationships, *people*, didn't distract him like this. He didn't allow them to.

The attitude he'd taken—let Jen go her own obstinate way and see how far it got her—had become somehow harder to stick to the moment the front door slammed behind her.

He was concerned about her.

Whatever else that kiss had meant, he didn't know. Wasn't sure he wanted to know. Concern was the first step on a slippery slope towards caring, and he no longer did that. But somewhere along the way they'd become friends, and he couldn't now just let this go. It hadn't been so bad at the ball. He'd been around to keep tabs on the situation. This was completely different. She was on her own.

Richard Moran was not just a ruthless businessman, he also had a very nasty accusation of sexual harassment lurking in his not-too-distant past. An accusation hastily dropped, yet rumoured to be true. And that was just one of many indicators of the unsavoury side of his personality.

Alex threw his cup into the sink and grabbed his keys. However things were between them, he should never have let Jen go today. He might as well have let her go swimming with a very hungry shark. She wouldn't thank him, he knew that, but anything would be better than sitting here driving himself nuts. He'd blag his way into the VIP enclosure when he got there.

The Christmas race meet was a jovial affair. The VIP enclosure was festooned with decorations in subtle shades of blue and aqua, perfectly co-ordinated. Spicy mulled cider and canapés were served in the warmth of the glass-fronted bar as horses thundered past outside, their breath clouding the frosty air.

After talking about himself for the entire car journey, Richard Moran seemed alarmingly determined to turn the tables on her as soon as they arrived. It was much harder to work the perfect date when you were constantly being kept on your toes about your fictional background.

The first person he introduced her to turned out to be a successful jewellery designer with her own exclusive studio and website. Jen felt a line of perspiration break out along her spine as Richard mentioned her own invented jewellery business, and then watched beadily as she tried not to squirm while fielding questions about what was and wasn't hot in jewellery right now.

As the afternoon progressed being with him felt more and more like walking on eggshells.

She'd no sooner pasted on a breezy smile as he introduced her to Annabel and Cosmo—'Old, old friends, darling. Cosmo and I studied together at Cambridge.'—than she was fighting back a wave of nausea as he pointed out that Annabel had attended the fictional private school she'd chosen.

'Prior Park College, wasn't it? You must have been there around the same time,' he said.

Annabel flicked back her glossy chestnut bob and surveyed her with perfectly made-up eyes.

'I don't remember you,' she said.

'Ah, well, it's a big school, isn't it? Perhaps we were there at different times.' Jen groped desperately for a way to change the subject.

'What house were you in?'

'Aha! Those canapés look delicious!' she gabbled.

She made a beeline for a waiter a few paces away and returned munching a port and stilton tartlet. She couldn't think of any other way of causing a diversion, and etiquette rules forbade her from speaking with her mouth full. She glanced at Richard and realised with a cold flash that she wasn't doing half as well as she'd thought she was. He gave her a penetrating look which made her nerves fray. She tried to stop the rising heat in her cheeks by force of the mind, certain that he would pick up on the slightest blush.

He was suspicious of her.

The friendly, upbeat façade had switched like lightning to coldness, and she felt a dark twinge of unease as she remembered Alex's warnings about him. She suddenly wished she'd heeded his advice and quit while she was ahead with the success of the ball to write about. But, no, she'd been so stupidly flattered by the in-your-face flowers and attention, and the idea of proving a point to Alex, that she'd failed to keep a clear head.

Her only option was to stick to her story and try to avoid being alone with him.

Richard drew Cosmo aside for a private discussion, and Annabel propelled Jen towards a group of glossy women who eyed her up and down as if she was some new and interesting life form. She took a deep breath. *Intimidated* didn't really cover it, but at least Richard was distracted.

'You can always count on Richard to bring along someone new.' Annabel gave a tinkly laugh.

Jen bit back a sarcastic reply. Yes, she knew he was a playboy—but surely it must be bad form to point that out?

She soon found that belittling the girlfriend of a rich bachelor was practically a sport in itself among these women.

'I had that dress, too—what a coincidence! It's darling, isn't it?'

Jen glanced at the skinny blonde woman, introduced to her as Sukie.

The three other women leaned backwards in unison and looked at her dress. As a spectator she might even have found it funny. She concentrated hard on keeping her posture relaxed.

'Thank you,' she said.

'Designer. Last season.'

Jen didn't miss the challenge. Pointing out that the dress wasn't brand-new was an underhand move. She didn't rise.

'Unfortunately I had a bit of an accident in mine,' Sukie said. 'Someone spilled red wine down it at a wedding back in January. Landed mainly on the hemline. I remember it flapping around my ankles all wet. I could never quite get the…' her voice trailed off '…stain out.'

If this had been a movie the camera would have moved in on Jen for an immediate close-up. She tried desperately to keep a dignified look on her face when what it wanted to do was fold in on herself. Four pairs of beady rich eyes swivelled downwards to the hem of her dress. Jen didn't need to glance down herself. She could tell just from their expressions what she would see if she did. The sweet floral print on the deep green fabric was busy enough for the stain to blend in on cursory checking. If you didn't know it was there you would miss it. Turned out, she had.

'I donated it to Oxfam,' Sukie added, to no one in particular. 'In Knightsbridge.'

So Sukie had no compunction about donating imperfect clothing to charity without pointing out the flaw. Jen really couldn't give a damn what someone like that thought about her. Her temper flared.

'I'm all for wearing second-hand clothing,' she said. 'Too much emphasis is placed on the price tag in my opinion. No one cares if it costs more than a car as long as it's by an in-vogue designer. It's incredibly shallow. And by the way…' she frowned at Sukie, who took a step backwards '…you were supposed to point out to the store that there's a stain on the dress.'

She realised that the elegant, quiet tone she'd consciously been trying to maintain had disappeared and her loud voice was making heads turn.

Richard Moran swiftly rejoined the group, tumbler of whisky in hand.

'What's going on?'

'Genevieve appears to be wearing one of Sukie's castoffs,' Annabel said smoothly, with that tinkly laugh again. 'I think she's finding the situation a little awkward, Richard.'

Jen's heart plummeted. Not one face in the group was friendly. They saw her as an impostor, and she supposed that was exactly what she was.

Richard Moran grabbed her by the elbow and pulled her aside.

'Do you want to tell me what's going on here?' he barked in a stage whisper. 'Your big talk about a jewellery business just doesn't stack up, you fobbed Annabel off when she asked about school and now it turns out your dress is from a charity shop. What are you? Some kind of stalker?'

Jen felt a hot flash of contempt at the way he was treating her. And he thought she was pursuing him because she was infatuated? How arrogant could you be?

'Don't be ridiculous.' She yanked her elbow free and snapped impulsively, 'I'm not a stalker. I'm a journalist!'

The words were barely out of her mouth before he'd grabbed her a second time, one arm clamped around her waist, the other digging sharply into her arm. The black eyes had a sinister tinge in them. He pulled her hard towards the roped-off exit.

She struggled. 'What are you doing? Let go of me.'

He clamped her against him and spoke with absolute clarity in her ear as he propelled her along. She was vaguely aware that he was simultaneously smiling and nodding at people as they passed. Keeping up appearances.

'You are going to walk out of here with me without making any fuss,' he hissed. 'We are going to go somewhere quiet and you are going to tell me exactly what you are up to and who you are working for.'

His grip bit bruisingly hard into her arm and she felt the first dark tendrils of real fright twisting their way through her. Her instincts told her Alex had been right. This was not a man to be trifled with. She forced her whirling mind to *think*. She needed to get herself away from Richard before he could find out any more about her. Thank goodness she'd used a false name. If she made a run for it there was no way he could trace her.

Gathering all her strength, she kicked him as hard as she could in the shins—but instead of releasing her he unclamped his hand from her arm and grabbed a handful of her hair. She struggled madly and drew in a huge breath to scream.

The sound died on her lips as Richard Moran lurched suddenly sideways. Letting go of her, he fell into a nearby dark blue spiral Christmas tree. She stumbled to keep her own balance. As he got to his feet, covered in blue glitter and dabbing the corner of his mouth with the back of his hand, she found herself dragged away at speed.

It was Alex.

He'd come, after all.

They barely spoke at first as the car sped back to London. Her emotions were in turmoil. Hideous disappointment at the failure of Mission Racing churned deep in her stomach along with the humiliation of being manhandled to the exit, VIP heads turning her way. The dreadful feeling of being frighteningly out of her depth was something she loathed. But underneath it all there was a tentative glimmering of deep-down happiness at what Alex's dramatic intervention might mean.

He'd bailed her out again. This time at huge cost to himself. Would he really do that for a potential one-night stand he never needed to cross paths with again?

Eventually she could stand it no longer.

'Thank you,' she said. 'For not saying it.'

'Saying what?'

She gave him a rueful smile.

'I told you so. The temptation must be huge.'

She saw the tension in his shoulders soften a little.

'It is,' he said.

Silence fell again.

'VIP tickets weren't as scarce as they made out, then,' she said. 'Seems a bit of a scam.'

'What?' He glanced at her.

'The auction,' she said. 'The other night. I almost got stung for a grand on supposedly gold-dust tickets, but you just strolled in like you owned the place.'

Strolled in was actually way off the mark. Vaulted into the fray was more like it.

He stared straight ahead.

'No big deal.'

'No big deal? You *hit* him! There were enough diamond-encrusted mobile phones in that VIP enclosure to guarantee you a place on tomorrow's front pages. You're probably already an internet sensation.'

'I don't care,' he said.

Her stomach gave a dizzying flip. Being rescued shouldn't really sit well with her lifelong determination to go it alone. And yet the deliciousness of it took her breath away.

They were almost at the apartment now.

'What about the movie? All your PR rules? You've probably broken every single one in the space of two minutes.' The grief this was likely to cause him suddenly hit home, and she felt a sickening stab of guilt at what she'd dragged him into.

'Yeah, well, I've spent my entire career worrying about how my every move affects my work, chasing success at the expense of everything else. Maybe I just decided to do what I want for a change, without reference to any of that.'

'So all this is about you making a point? Nothing more?'

'What do you mean?'

'All this…' She waved her hands in an all-encompassing gesture. 'Everything you've done. Gatecrashing the racing.'

He pulled the car to a standstill in his apartment's parking space, turned the engine off, got out. She followed him into the lobby, waiting for an answer.

'Come on,' she said. 'Am I just a distraction because you've been forced to stay in and miss the party for a few lousy weeks? What's this all about?'

He stopped, laughed into the darkness.

'A distraction?' he said. 'You're right. I've never been so distracted by anything or anyone. And it has nothing to do with my PR team or the award prospects for my damn movie.'

In two quick strides he was right back beside her. Her stomach melted into softness.

'I should never have let you go with him today.'

'Then why did you?'

'Because you were so determined to prove a point, and you would have argued me down until you were blue in the face.'

He looked up at the ceiling briefly.

'And because I didn't want to admit how much I want you.'

Heat tingled through her as he slid one hand firmly around her waist, traced the other along her collarbone. Sparks jolted deliciously down her spine.

'Since when?'

He smiled down at her.

'To be honest I think I was halfway there the first

night—just finding you in the apartment like that, with your long legs and all that attitude. But I think what really sealed it was the orange hair.'

All sense and rationality left her, pushed out by the intensity of the desire that rushed through her under his touch. She let her arms circle his neck, let his thick hair slide through her fingers. The green depths of his gaze met her own. She felt as if her knees had melted and might quit holding her up very soon.

'I could always dye it back,' she said into his mouth, and she felt the grin on his lips as he kissed her, his hands sliding lower to press her hard against him.

She felt him tighten his hold enough to lift her and then he was walking down the hall, her toes skimming the floor in the semi-darkness. She heard him mash the key blindly into the lock as he kissed her hungrily. Then, as he carried her inside and kicked the door shut behind him, all reservation was gone. She locked her legs behind his waist and let him carry her through to his bedroom.

Sunlight slanted into the room through a chink in the heavy curtains and fell on the pillow next to Jen, pulling her back to consciousness. Alex's side of the bed was empty. She slid her hand beneath the cover.

Still warm.

She glanced around, collecting her thoughts. The room was pure Alex, like the rest of the apartment. Nothing personal or sentimental. No indication that he'd put down roots here. It felt like sleeping in a hotel room. A very expensive one. A full flashback of what had happened between them zoomed into her mind and she threw the sheets back quickly.

The deep feeling of hot euphoria that had enveloped her very bones at the feel of him the previous night was fast

regressing into cold tension. She stood up, glanced round
the room for her clothes. Her panties had somehow ended
up under the chest of drawers, and she hooked them out
and stepped into them.

What had she done?

Carried away by her very own Sir Galahad, stepping
in yet again to save her. Was that what had removed her
sanity? The novelty of having someone actually *be* there
for her for a change, for her to rely on? She'd told herself
she was happy with her life, yet there had always been
that sniff of what might have been lingering just out of
her reach. Hell, that was what had driven the whole article
idea. Had she let him under her radar because he repre-
sented that parallel universe for her—the one where she
really was a rich socialite instead of just playing a part?

Rationality was sinking in deeper with every moment,
driving away the delicious feeling of happiness she'd en-
countered in his arms, with his hands on her skin.

She could hear his muffled voice somewhere outside
the room and paused near the door, listening hard. He was
obviously on the telephone. That meant he could be back
in here at any moment. She looked hurriedly around for
the rest of her clothes and suddenly registered a swatch
of dialogue.

'…tomorrow. Send me the flight details through…'

Cold regret seeped into her heart as she followed what
he was saying. Along with anger at herself for letting
things go so far.

Where exactly had she *thought* it would go from here?
She knew what his priorities were. He hadn't made a secret
of it. Work came first. Would always come first with him.

Flight details.

So he wasn't even staying in the country for Christmas,
then? What would he give her? A couple of days before

he jetted off back to his life? What had she been thinking? She'd fallen into his arms like some simpering idiot, all because he'd rescued her from a scary situation. She'd slept with him and now he was going.

The only thing stopping her from becoming her mother right now was the fact he'd used a condom.

She dashed around the room, picking up her dress and cardigan. Now reality had bitten she knew only that she had to put a stop to any further repeat of history. There was only one way forward if she were to retain the control her mother had given up.

She'd have to dump him before he got in first.

CHAPTER TEN

ALEX returned to the bedroom via the kitchen fridge, thinking they would have a slow and languorous champagne-
breakfast-fuelled second round. Just the thought of the
warm softness of her body curled up in his bed made hot
desire rush through him again.

The bed was empty, sheets strewn haphazardly across it.
As he glanced at the half-open *en suite* bathroom door, of
the darkness beyond it, she popped up suddenly from behind the far side of the bed. She was naked except for lace
panties and clutching the rest of her clothes to her chest,
hiding her modesty as if he *hadn't* just spent half the night
exploring every silken inch of her body. He stared at her.

'What are you doing?'

She avoided his eyes, bent down and retrieved a shoe
from under the bed.

'I need to get going.'

He shoved the tray down on the chest of drawers as she
moved towards him. On her way out.

'To do what, exactly?'

'I need to get to work. This article won't write itself.'

'Come back to bed. Have some breakfast. Another hour
isn't going to make a difference.'

'Well, if that's your attitude I'm amazed you've made

such a success of your career,' she said. 'Lying in bed until all hours.'

'It's only seven-thirty,' he pointed out.

She was next to him now, next to the open door, shoes balanced on top of her clothes. She apparently really was going.

'So you're choosing work over a lie-in with me?' Surely she couldn't be serious. 'Let's just have something to eat and then you can get started, spend the day on it. You can use the office, if you like.'

'I don't need to use the office. I need to get packed and then I'll be out of your hair.'

His mind whirled. What the hell *was* this?

'Out of my hair?'

She shrugged.

'It's been fun, but we both knew it was never going anywhere…right?'

He didn't answer. He was too busy trying to fathom how things had gone from the intimate sizzling passion of the night to this detached coldness.

Not bothering to wait for an answer, she finally pushed past him and walked barefoot down the hall towards her own room, still clutching her clothes against her. He followed her, the smooth contours of her naked back tantalising him. Messy waves of hair were tumbling every which way over her shoulders.

She talked loudly without looking round. 'Won't take me long to get my stuff sorted.'

'You're moving out?'

'Yes, our agreement's reached an end. I told you I needed to stay until I got enough material. I've done that.' She paused. 'It's over.'

She walked into her room, made as if to close the door. He grabbed it and stood in the way.

'But you haven't written it yet.'

'Oh, I can write the thing anywhere,' she said. 'I've got all my notes. Once it's done I'll just e-mail it in and hope it's good enough. I'm going to see my mum.'

'You're going home to the country?'

'For Christmas,' she said. She turned. Faced him. 'Let's face it, Alex, I was always going to be going home to the country for Christmas. This can't come as a big surprise.'

'But last night…'

'Was great. But you're not exactly the marrying kind, are you?'

She smiled at him, as if she was perfectly fine with that, but it was a perfunctory effort and didn't really touch the blue eyes. He'd seen what a proper smile looked like on her face and this was a poor imitation. Whatever was going on here, he wasn't buying it.

'I've got ambitions,' she said. 'There's a lot riding on this project for me. I don't have time to take a few more days out for sex with you just because you're stuck here and you happen to have an empty diary.'

That was all it was to her? Sex? He couldn't believe what he was hearing.

'Let's just cut our losses and get back to normal. You must be going back to work any day now, anyway, aren't you?'

There was a loaded tone to that question, a hint of contempt. Or maybe he'd imagined it.

He dropped his eyes for a moment, but there was no point trying to hide it.

'I do have to fly out to the States,' he admitted. 'My spat with Richard Moran is going to be plastered all over the papers for the next day or so, but my PR team will smooth it over. We're well known as business rivals, and it isn't the first time we've crossed swords, so they'll pass it off as a long-running feud and your name shouldn't come into it.' He gave her a small smile. 'And even if it does it won't be your real name.'

'Good,' she said. She didn't smile back. 'So I've become Viveca Holt. You sleep with me, there's a scandal in the press and you make yourself scarce. History repeats itself.'

'What happened with Viveca has nothing to do with this. Don't you think I'd stay here if I could? Ride out the storm with you? There's been a hitch with the funding for one of my films—the kind of thing I don't want to leave to anyone else to sort out. That's the reason I have to go. I need to get back in control. I've been gone long enough.'

That urge to be back in charge was as strong as ever. He had a hands-on involvement in every film. Delegation didn't come naturally. He found it hard to believe anyone else had the commitment and standards that he did. And yet now he found it tempered by the want, the *need* to be with her.

'When?' she asked, matter-of-fact.

'Tomorrow,' he said.

'Well, there you go, then!'

He clenched his hands at her sudden dismissive attitude.

'It's the States, Jen. It's not the moon. I'm not disappearing off the face of the earth. There are phones. There's Skype. And I'll be back.'

'Of course you will. Next time your work demands it. I'm sure I'll read about it in the papers.'

Her tone was don't-care.

She turned her back on him, dropped the ball of clothes on the bed and stood momentarily naked except for her panties, shrugging her way as fast as she could into a T-shirt. He could be across the room with her in three quick strides, sliding his hands around her to cup her breasts, kissing the back of her neck. It took huge will-power not to do exactly that, to use sex in that way he was used to—to divert a woman from anything with more depth and importance. But he didn't go. He didn't know where he wanted this…this *thing* between them to go, but he suddenly realised he wanted more from her than just sex. And to pitch them at that level now would, he instinctively knew, be a huge mistake.

Now wearing T-shirt and panties, she hauled a suitcase out from under her bed and crossed the room to the bureau, pulling open drawers, gathering up clothes and belongings. He crossed the room and shut the lid of her suitcase, stood between it and her.

'Will you quit packing for a minute?'

She took a deep breath and stood still, a T-shirt in each hand. Her expression was one of sad resignation and his heart lurched.

'I don't want this to be it between us. Don't you understand?' he said. He made an effort to curb his tone. In his determination to make her understand his temper was fraying. 'I know the situation isn't perfect. We've both got huge demands on us, on our time. But I want to carry on seeing you.'

'For what? A couple of dates? Or are you after an easy date whenever you happen to be in town? Call me up and I'll drop everything and be there? Is that it?'

'Jen, I know why you're acting like this. You're cutting me out because you think you know me. You're judging me, judging *us*, by a million stories you've read about me in the press. And that's not fair. I'm serious about this. Don't you think you at least owe me the chance to show you that?'

She looked at him, eyebrows raised.

'How do you plan to do that?'

He thought her tone had warmed up slightly, almost imperceptibly. Maybe at last he was getting through to her.

He took a deep breath. He couldn't quite believe what he was about to suggest.

'I fly out tomorrow to LA. Spend today with me. And at the end of it, if you still want out, I won't argue with you. Your damn article can wait one day.'

'You think spending one day in bed with you is enough to convince me you're serious about me?'

'Not you, no,' he said. 'But then you're not run-of-the-mill, are you? Get showered and dressed. We're going out.'

'The M4?'

She glanced at the motorway sign. The main route to her home village.

'I thought you were talking me out of going home. Trust me, my mother won't thank me for turning up out of the blue with a guest in tow. She'll be up to her elbows in pastry, making the famous Brown mince pies. Or, worse, she could be stuffing the turkey.'

'The M4 doesn't just serve Littleford, you know,' he said, not taking his eyes off the road.

Light snow was falling against the windscreen, but it was deliciously snug in the Maserati with its seat-warming gadgetry and perfect climate control.

She caught on.

'We're going to Bristol?'

'We're visiting my parents,' he said. 'The Hammond Christmas drinks and nibbles. You'd better brace yourself.'

Jen sat in silence as he took the Bristol slip road, mulling over what this could mean. She'd challenged him with this, hadn't she? With taking her to meet his family? Was Alex proving a point? Nervous butterflies pinged around her stomach.

It seemed the bonkers British weather hadn't put off the traditional last-minute rush of Christmas shoppers. The roads to the town centre were stuffed with traffic, which finally began to ease as they headed for the Downs and Clifton.

'I should warn you they're likely to be a bit narky,' he said as he pulled the car into a wide avenue lined with snow-dusted trees. They came to a standstill outside a beautiful three-storey townhouse. 'On account of the fact I haven't visited for a while.'

She crunched across the frozen gravel driveway behind him. He rang the bell.

'How long is "a while"?' she asked as the front door opened and a man stepped into view.

Alex shrugged. 'Eighteen months-ish.'

'More like two years,' the man said.

He had to be Alex's father. The resemblance was strong. Sixty-ish, he had the same thick hair, though it was steel-grey, and glasses. Alex had his green eyes.

And then they were surrounded. Alex's mother appeared from nowhere, petite with a short light brown haircut to match her elfin features. Alex made an apologetic face at Jen over her head as she dragged him into an enormous hug. There was a brother, there was a small niece and nephew who hung off Alex's legs, there was a grandma sitting in a high-backed chair by the fireplace, and there were uncles, aunts and cousins. A total of four generations of the Hammond family.

Cheesy Christmas music was belting out from somewhere within.

The rich exterior of the house didn't match the inside. It was stuffed to breaking point with mismatched furniture and no surface was left uncluttered. There were ornaments and knick-knacks everywhere she looked.

'I bought them the house seven years ago,' Alex said as they were ushered through the hall. 'Not long after I got my first big break. Took me ages to persuade them to move out of their old house, and when they eventually did they told my interior designer to get stuffed and basically moved the interior of their old place as it was.'

In the corner of the sitting room there was an enormous fake Christmas tree, festooned with a combination of hideous baubles and homemade ornaments that spelled the word *family* in a way that nothing else at Christmas quite did. A threadbare fairy perched on the top, well past her best but clearly there for years to come based on sentimentality instead of appearance.

Alex was subjected to an inquisition from the entire family that he clearly deserved and took calmly in his stride.

'Good of you to finally show your face,' his father said when they'd been each been given a glass of cranberry-red Christmas punch.

Yep, there was definitely an air of narkiness.

'I've invited you and Mum to visit me in LA loads of times,' Alex protested. 'Tried to persuade you to come and have a holiday. You never take me up on it.'

'You know your mother is afraid of flying. And I don't hold with that foreign food. It doesn't agree with me.'

Everywhere Jen looked there were framed pictures of Alex with his younger brother, growing up. There was an enormous table groaning with quiche, sausage rolls and sandwiches. Good hearty food, not the one-bite-and-it's-gone canapés she'd been served these last few weeks.

The argument went on.

'Would it kill you to phone your mother once a week? Or even once a month? I know your every move, Alexander Hammond, I read the red-top newspapers. I know when you're in this country, skulking in London, not bothering to nip down the M4 for an hour or so to see your family. And then just this morning there's a picture of you smacking someone at some racetrack. Off the rails! Are you on drugs?'

Alex held both hands up to ward him off.

'No, I am not on drugs! And I was staying out of the way because I wanted to protect you lot from all that.' He turned to Jen. 'The press hounded them when I broke up with Susan,' he explained. 'They'd follow my mother when she walked down the street, barking out questions.' He looked at his parents. 'I didn't want that for you again.'

'We've taken more grief than that in our time,' his mother snapped. 'When our Michael got caught shoplifting I couldn't hold my head up in the supermarket for weeks. A few gutter press weren't going to bother me after that.'

'What's shoplifting, Daddy?' Alex's six-year-old niece piped up.

Michael threw his hands up. 'Oh, cheers, Mum. Trying to be a role model here and you bring that up.'

As the day progressed and the punchbowl emptied things slowly began to thaw. As darkness fell Jen stood in a corner of the warm kitchen watching Alex deep in conversation with his father and brother.

'You're the first girlfriend he's brought home in a long time,' his mother said, joining her. She topped up Jen's glass, then her own.

'I'm sure it's just because work keeps him away so much.'

A pause and an unconvinced smile.

'Come and let me show you something.'

Jen followed her out of the kitchen.

There was an enormous ball of mistletoe suspended from the doorway into the sitting room, and Alex's eccentric uncle Norman seemed to be hanging around it rather more than necessary. He flashed her a toothy smile as she sidled past him into the room.

'I'm amazed to see him,' Alex's mother said as they sat down on the sofa. 'He has no need for us any more. We're lucky to get a phone call now and then. He's got all he needs—all those rich friends. There's nothing here that he wants to come back for.'

Jen shook her head. 'You're wrong. He misses you. He misses *this*.'

She was fascinated. It had always been just her and her mum. Her grandparents were long gone. She envied him the warmth, the buzz of it. You'd never be on your own with a family like this.

Unless you took yourself out of it. Which was what he had done.

'I've kept all the cuttings from his career.'

She produced a groaning photo album. Jen forced her face to keep a smile on it as she flipped through a few pages. It was full of tabloid pictures of Alex with various models and starlets. Here was Alex on the red carpet with a gorgeous redhead. And here he was cavorting in the surf somewhere tropical, with Viveca Holt of all people.

Photos of ex-girlfriends. Exactly what you needed to boost your ailing confidence when you met the parents for the first time. *Not.*

'Fabulous!' she exclaimed, smiling so hard her cheeks ached. 'And have you seen all his films?'

'Oh, yes,' she said. 'We've got all the DVDs.'

Alex's mother leaned in conspiratorially and added in a stage whisper, 'Some of them are a bit dull, to be perfectly honest, a bit too arty for us. Still, I'd never tell him that. It's brilliant that he's won all those awards. Graham and I prefer more of an action film, like that *Faith* trilogy. We love those—have you seen them?'

As they said their goodbyes Alex bandied about promises of regular visits and phone calls. In the silent warmth of the car on the drive back to London Jen wondered if he'd meant them. Or whether the whole day had really been about proving a point.

CHAPTER ELEVEN

Rule #8: When you've snared your millionaire, gradually introduce him to the real you one step at a time.

'Why did you take me to meet them?'

Alex stared into the fireplace for a moment. She was curled warmly against him on the sofa in the den, back in his apartment. The room was lit only by the soft glow of the fire and the coloured lights on her little Christmas tree. She followed his gaze, watched sparks flying from the logs into the velvety darkness. Two glasses of wine and the remains of scrambled eggs on toast lay on the coffee table to the side of them.

'I wanted to show you my roots,' he said. 'You were so determined to accept the newspaper view of me as a playboy, and I don't blame you. I've never tried to correct it either publicly or privately. To be honest I haven't cared either way what was written about me.' He glanced at her. 'Not until now.'

'Why now?' Her heart beat faster as she waited for his reply.

'I want you to know what I'm really like. Not the press image. The real me. If you're going to do a bunk I want it to be because you're not happy with *me*, not some illusion.'

'Why haven't you seen them for so long?' she asked. 'They were so delighted to see you I thought you were going to be lynched, and you obviously love them all to bits.'

He took a sip of his wine.

'Part of it was the demands of work keeping me away. I wasn't lying to them about that. But it isn't the only reason.'

He sighed.

'After Susan left it was just such a reminder of what I was missing, seeing them all. My brother became a dad, something I could never see happening for me after she went, and it became easier somehow to just stay away. They've never been excited by what I do. Not when I was a kid starting out and not even when I became a success at it. Michael's given them grandchildren. He sees them all the time. Those are things they can relate to. His life is real to them.'

He ran a hand distractedly through his hair.

'I think they see me in the newspapers and wonder who the hell I am. When I see them they act like I think I'm better than them. I sometimes think they'd have been happier if I drove a taxi for a living or worked down at the docks.'

She could see his agitation in the tensing of his shoulders and was touched. If today had been about proving to her he was serious, it hadn't been an easy gesture for him to make.

'But what conclusion did you *want* them to make? You've encouraged them to think that way by staying away so much. They think you're ashamed of them because you don't see them.'

He flinched, and she knew she'd touched a nerve, but she wasn't about to back down.

'I can see where you're coming from,' she said. 'They're happy in their own little bubble. Flying halfway round the world fills them with dread. But it isn't that they aren't proud of you. It's just that they're so in awe of the world you live in.'

He was shaking his head. She put a hand on his arm.

'Your parents own all your films, you know,' she said. 'They've got them all, every single one, on DVD. I saw. And your mum subjected me to a scrapbook of newspaper clippings. You in the arms of half of Hollywood. I was expecting baby photos and I got you frolicking in the surf with Viveca Holt. They're your biggest fans, you idiot. Just because they don't really understand what you do it doesn't mean they aren't proud of your achievements.'

A pause. He watched the fire.

'Maybe,' he said.

'You should see more of them.'

'I know.'

'That Christmas tree is a shrine to your childhood,' she said.

He grimaced.

'I know. It's hideous. Sorry.'

She shook her head. 'No, I like it. That's the kind of Christmas tree I want to have one day. You can keep those ludicrous black trees with minimalist lights and those deconstructed turkey dinners. It's like wearing designer clothes and not caring if you look like a moose as long as they cost a fortune. Christmas at your parents' has been fine-tuned over years and years. It actually has something concrete behind it instead of vacuous self-importance.'

'So your Christmas tree will be festooned with tat?'

'Decorations made by toddlers do not fall into the *tat* category.'

He laughed, gave her a squeeze.

'I thought you were aiming for editor-in-chief of Vogue.'

His tone was neutral, almost deliberately so. 'How are you going to fit family in with that?'

'This isn't the Dark Ages. I know you think it's impossible to mix business with family life but I don't agree. I definitely want kids one day. You just need to be good at juggling and working as a team. Women are fabulous at that kind of thing.' She pointed an emphatic finger at him. 'Your big problem is you think it has to be all or nothing. Anything less than white-picket-fence-two-kids-and-a-dog-perfection doesn't cut it for you. But, like I told you before, there's more than one way to crack a nut. As long as both parents are never away for work at the same time, maybe downsize their hours a bit, delegate more, cut down on travelling. There's loads of ways you could make it work.' She leaned forward, picked up her wine glass and took a sip. 'I intend to have it all. Nothing's going to stop me.'

'I guess I thought the way things were with your father and your insane sense of ambition, that you weren't big on family.'

'I'm not right now. But give me a few years working my way up and family is next up.' She paused. 'My father is irrelevant.'

He glanced her way. 'Is he?'

She leaned against him for a moment, savouring the warmth of him, the feeling of security his closeness gave.

'Almost doing a bunk this morning was about me, too,' she said. 'Not just about you.'

He moved sideways a little so he could see her face.

'It's not you, it's me?' he said, eyebrows raised. 'You don't have to spare my feelings. I just want you to be honest with me.'

'Remember when we talked about false names for my article and you suggested I use my father's surname?'

He frowned.

'Yes.'

'Well, the fact he's a waste of space wasn't the only reason I didn't use it. I didn't want to draw attention.'

'How do you mean?'

She took a deep breath.

'My father is Dominic Armstrong.'

She waited. The fire spat softly in the background.

'You don't mean *the* Dominic Armstrong? The—'

'The media giant,' she finished for him. 'Yes.'

He looked sharply down at her, his interest clearly buzzing. Of course it was. She met his gaze, ready for the questions.

'But he owns two or three newspapers, doesn't he? Not to mention magazines and that TV news channel?'

'He does.'

'Then I don't get it. All it would take is a bit of name-dropping and you could land yourself a job on the magazine of your choice. But instead you've slogged your way up with an internship after working for a newspaper from the back of beyond.'

'It's how I wanted it. I've never wanted to be indebted to him for anything. Twenty-five years and not a card. Not a phone call. The only part he's ever played in my life was on his way out of it. He had my mother sign a contract—gave her a lump sum in return for relinquishing all parental responsibility.'

'He paid her off?' He sounded appalled.

'Exactly. And that's why I was trying to make a quick exit this morning. Because when you get down to basics he saw me and my mother as a hitch in his life. So he fixed the problem and then disappeared.' She paused. 'Like you did with Viveca Holt.'

'You're comparing *me* to your father?'

She could hear the edge in his voice, grabbed his hand, held it.

'Not now. But I was this morning.'

He'd pulled away from her, a frown touching his brows. She spoke quickly, needing to make him understand.

'Think about how it looked to me. You had an affair with Viveca, it began to cause you problems in the media, so you got your PR people onto it and got the hell out of the country. And then we spent the night together, you're plastered across the press for belting Richard Moran in the chops—a situation caused by me—and suddenly your PR people are on the case and you're jetting off to LA. What was I supposed to think? I wanted to jump before I was pushed. I don't want to make the same mistakes my mother did.'

He took her face softly in his hands, looked steadily into her eyes. The woody scent of the fire mingled with the fresh citrus of his aftershave.

'This is not a mistake. I am not getting on a plane to fly out of your life. Don't judge me by the way your father behaved.'

'I couldn't help it. After twenty-five years it gets to be a bit of a mind-set.'

'Give me time and I'll change that.'

He pulled her against him in the firelight, held her, kissed her so deeply it made her light-headed, and then he was easing her onto his lap, his hands sliding deliciously beneath her clothes, and she let hot desire for him crush away doubt.

Afterwards she lay in his arms, watched the fire flicker. He grabbed the patchwork throw from the armchair and tugged it around them.

'You really think this can work?'

She wondered where they could go from here. Would he suggest that she move her work ambitions across the pond? Or even drop them altogether? Take on a new job as Alex Hammond's Other Half? With his views on putting each other first, surely that was how he would see things progressing. Susan had supposedly left him because he wasn't in the same room as her often enough, so chances were he'd view working on different continents as a bit of a hitch.

She looked up at him to gauge his response and he kissed her forehead gently.

'Yes, I really think this can work.'

'With you on the other side of the Atlantic?'

She waited.

'You could come with me, you know,' he said.

There it was.

She wriggled away enough to raise herself on an elbow. The glow from the fire lit the strong contours of his face. His green eyes held her gaze and her heart turned over softly. There was a part of her that wanted to leap in immediately, agree to anything he asked just to keep him. But the self-sufficient part of her, honed over twenty-five years, easily held its own.

'I can't do that,' she said, and waited for it all to begin unravelling.

'I didn't think so,' he said, 'which is why I'll be relying on air travel.'

'Air travel?' Her heart did a happy little skip.

'When you get this new job—'

'*If,*' she interrupted.

'OK, *if* you get this new job, you're going to be even more career-obsessed than you are now, right?'

'Obsessed is going a bit far,' she said, and then saw his raised eyebrows. She sighed. 'Maybe you have a point.'

'And I'm not going to lie to you, my work schedule can be fierce. I've built it up to be exactly that. It's been everything for me these last few years. I can't downsize my hours overnight.'

'I wouldn't expect you to.'

'But I could start to rebuild things from now—work my schedule so it fits with yours. We both work hard when we're apart, and we make the most of every moment we're together. Starting now.'

He slid his hands beneath the throw and turned with her so she was on her back, the softness of the velvet sofa against her naked skin as he loomed above her. He leaned down to kiss the line of her collarbone, sending sparks fizzing right down to her toes, and then moved back up to look into her eyes, his forehead pressed lightly against hers, his warm breath on her mouth.

'I'm serious about this,' he said. 'I'm serious about you. And even though I'm as scared of letting people close as you are, a few thousand miles aren't about to stop me.'

Perfect man, perfect Christmas. And now New Year, new job.

She straightened her new short jacket. Now she had a proper regular income and an image to keep up. She had money for clothes. Not the designer level stuff she'd bought to play Genevieve, but a wardrobe that was a cut above her old jeans-and-T-shirt uniform. Marlon's makeover had been all about playing a part for her article, but somewhere along the way she'd begun to like feeling a bit more polished.

Plus she wanted to look her best for Alex. He'd managed two visits since Christmas—one a four-day break and the other a forty-eight-hour turnaround spent almost entirely in bed that made her toes curl and her stomach melt whenever she thought about it. He called every day, and used Skype whenever he could, but she was still competing for his attention with film stars and models, and a new suit seemed *essential* under the circumstances.

She stacked her papers together and put them away in her briefcase, shook her editor's hand. The delicious feeling of having made it hadn't gone away yet. Four weeks in and she was still in pinch-yourself mode.

She'd done it. Actually done it. Sold her article to *Gossip!* magazine and been offered a permanent role in the Features Department. She was on her way. She'd just finished a meeting at which she'd pitched new article ideas and the reception had been great.

Her editor accompanied her down the hallway, a sheaf of papers in one arm.

'Really pleased to have you on board,' she said. 'Always on the lookout for a fresh approach.'

'I'm just so happy to have the opportunity.'

'No need to thank me.' She shifted the papers to the other arm. 'You came highly recommended, after all.'

Jen frowned. What the hell did *that* mean?

'Recommended? By who?'

No one at the *Littleford Gazette* had an ounce of clout in this universe. Maybe if she'd gone for a job with *Pig-Farming Monthly...*

'Our Entertainment Editor.' She smiled at Jen. 'Apparently Alex Hammond mentioned you to her a few weeks ago. The film producer. I had no idea you knew him. He gave her an exclusive interview on account of the fact you now work here. Fantastic scoop for her. She was delighted. That's exactly the kind of networking we should be doing.'

They'd reached Reception, the lifts. The editor gave Jen

a parting smile and she returned it automatically, oblivious to her surroundings, her mind working overtime.

Disbelief came first.

He wouldn't have done that. He knew how she felt about that article, how hard she'd worked, how she'd spent everything on it—not just in money terms. He wouldn't have undermined all that by pulling strings and namedropping.

Would he?

She didn't notice the other people in the lift as she descended to the ground floor. Didn't register anyone she passed.

It was in his nature to manipulate situations to get the outcome he wanted. She knew that much. Life had moulded him that way. He had all his staff sign confidentiality agreements. When they'd first met he'd tried to buy her off to get her out of his apartment. He paid a PR company to manipulate his image in the press. And he'd slept with Viveca Holt who, not so coincidentally, had then managed to get the showbiz break of her life. The list was endless. He wasn't above throwing money or influence at any situation to get the desired result. Why would this be any different?

Maybe he was too used to it after Susan's betrayal to act in any other way. Why leave anything to chance when you could manipulate the outcome?

Her mobile phone rang. She checked the screen. As if he had some sixth sense, it was Alex. She pressed 'call reject.'

Rule #9: If it doesn't work out, don't be downhearted. Have a Plan B. Go it alone and get rich and successful yourself.

Six missed calls and now she knew why. She'd forgotten the date.

She watched the annual award nominations as they were read out on the news channel. It was a good year for British film.

The Audacity of Death had eight nominations. One of them was Best Actress for Viveca Holt.

Hot anger boiled through her.

His success. His glory. No one else's. He could bask in his achievements, knowing his full worth, knowing they were down to him. His management, his drive.

He'd stolen that feeling from her. What meaning did her job have now?

The phone rang again and she answered it on autopilot, still looking at the TV screen.

'Hey,' he said.

His voice. The voice she loved. She lay awake at night waiting to hear it, just so she could go to sleep with it resonating in her mind.

'Hi.'

'Have you seen the news?' he asked.

'Eight nominations. Congratulations.'

He hadn't managed to screw things up, after all. Whatever publicity his exploits before Christmas had generated, it hadn't done the movie any harm.

'Will you come to the ceremony with me?' he asked.

Before she'd gone to work this morning that question would have filled her with excitement and delight. Not just at the prospect of attending what had to be one of the most glitzy evenings on any social calendar anywhere but because he wanted to share that event, that huge achievement, with *her*. It would have given her that happy little tummy-flip you got when the fabulous new boyfriend with whom you were totally smitten suggested you booked a holiday for later in the year. That insecurity-crushing fact you could repeat in your head at confidence crisis moments:

He intends to still be with me for the awards ceremony. He's serious about me. She would have been able to say that to herself in those moments when she missed him.

Instead she felt numb, as if all her senses had been wrapped in cotton wool.

'I can't, I'm afraid. I'll be working.'

There was a long pause. He was probably wondering if he'd heard correctly.

'This is a bad line. What did you say?'

'I said I'll be too busy,' she repeated. Speaking to him seemed to have opened the door on her pent-up anger. Just ajar at the moment, but it wouldn't take much for it to swing wide and bury her. 'Work's really taken off, and you know how I've given everything to get where I am. In fact, I'm not sure a relationship is the right thing for me just at the moment.'

'Jen, what the hell is this about?' His voice was strong in her ear, confusion and anger tingeing the edges.

Good. Let him be confused and angry. Just like her.

Her heart felt as if it was disintegrating. He wanted a woman he could control. He'd made her think he wanted to get close, maybe he'd even believed that himself, but in reality he'd been busy cobbling safety nets, making sure their life would be perfect, heading off anything that might cause a problem or challenge their happiness.

She didn't want that. She wanted to stand and fall on her own merits. To share her successes with him and lean on him through her failures. Would life with him just be one long cushioned ride? She wanted to *feel* life, the ups as well as the downs, taking whatever it threw at her head on. And she couldn't do that with him.

'You pulled strings at *Gossip!* magazine to swing me that job,' she said.

His silence on the end of the phone told her all she needed to know.

'Jen, listen to me,' he said at last. She could hear the urgency in his voice. 'It wasn't like that. You're reading too much into it.'

'You're saying you *didn't* promise an exclusive interview to *Gossip!* while I was staying with you at the apartment? While I was busting a gut, busting everything I had, to nail that job *on my own merit*?'

A long pause. She waited.

'I did promise them an interview, yes,' he said quietly. 'But it was not some calculated move to get them to accept your article. I know how much that job means to you, I know how hard you worked. Do you really think I would openly do something to jeopardise that?'

'I don't think you can help yourself,' she said. 'You have all this money, all this power, and you look at life and think about how you want this or that situation to turn out. And then you sort it. You went to *Gossip!* bandying my name about and offering an exclusive, and you expect me to believe you didn't ask for anything in return? You said it yourself at that Christmas ball—in this world it's all about knowing the right people, about greasing palms. Well, I can't live like that. I can't be with you like that. Catching me when I fall is one thing, but you'd have me living in a damn great safety harness.'

'You're not listening to me.'

'I don't need to listen to any more of this. What could you possibly say that can undo this? It's over, Alex.'

She hung up before she could break down. Waited for the phone to ring, for him to text, steeling herself to ignore him, not expecting for a moment that he would let things lie. Not Alex, who was used to getting his own way in everything.

The phone stayed silent.

Grief began to seep in alongside her anger. He was going to accept what she'd told him this time, without trying to manipulate what he wanted from the situation.

Maybe he was finally getting to understand her, after all. Now that it was too late.

CHAPTER TWELVE

SIXTEEN-HOUR days had kept Alex sane when his marriage had ended, and throwing himself into work now had its advantages. Funding was secured on three new films, and publicity for *The Audacity of Death* was frenzied. He tried to convince himself that his relationship with Jen had been a stupid mistake. A reminder that life for him worked best when he lived it alone. He turned back to the solace of work, the one focus that had always driven him, always given him a purpose, even in the face of Susan's betrayal.

And now it wasn't enough.

Somehow he'd managed to fall for her in a way he'd never fallen for anyone. Even Susan felt like a distant wisp of a memory now. The way she'd fleeced him had tortured him for the last five years and yet now it failed to raise so much as a stab of resentment. Work had slipped from being inspiring and satisfying to being nothing more than a way of occupying his mind, of shutting out the constant ache for her. What had she done to him? He could barely feel anything any more.

Dozens of times he went for the phone. He needed to hear her voice, to try and convince her how sorry he was. But he couldn't call her because she had been right.

He'd agreed to the interview with *Gossip!* while he'd waited for her during her makeover at Marlon's salon, thinking it might raise her profile a little at the magazine, smooth the way a bit for her. He hadn't done anything to actively pull strings. But there was no point denying he'd probably had some influence. Mentioning that Jen was connected to him was never going to do her any harm, was it? Just as it hadn't done Viveca any harm at the casting for *The Audacity of Death*. But while Viveca had been more than happy to take any opportunity that came her way, for Jen opportunity had to be made by *her*, not dropped in her lap.

He knew that now because he knew her better. They'd talked about her father, her past. He understood her single-minded ambition, her need to prove herself. But that had been later, when they were together. And by then the damage was done.

And now, more than a month on, work and the bachelor lifestyle were still not enough to block out the ache for her. He wasn't sure they ever would be again.

'Settling in OK?'

Jen turned from the counter. The coffee house was just around the corner from *Gossip!* HQ and she was addicted. No more Littleford Tea Rooms for her.

Angela West. Entertainment Editor. Whippet-thin. Super-intimidating designer suit. Jen had learned more about designer clobber in a couple of weeks living with Alex than she had in a lifetime in Littleford.

Oh, but it hurt to think about Alex. There was a raw ache deep inside her at the thought of never seeing him again, never being held by him again. In any other break-up situation throwing herself into work might have helped take her mind off it, but every move she made in the office was a bitter reminder of his betrayal. The constant wondering about whether she deserved this job at all crushed any joy she had in her work.

He'd not only broken her heart, he'd taken away the one thing that might have helped her get over it.

'Great, thanks,' she said. She took her full-fat latte and sprinkled it liberally with chocolate shavings. Added a white chocolate muffin to her tray. At least now she didn't have to worry about her weight or her skin breaking out, since she intended never to get naked with another man. *Ever.*

'And how's the fabulous Alex Hammond?' Angela asked, peering through the display cabinet glass, probably in search of something with zero calories. A plain rice cake, perhaps.

Jen felt as if she had been doused with cold water. Of course. Entertainment Editor. The penny dropped. The string Alex had pulled had apparently been attached to *her.*

'I haven't spoken to him recently,' she said vaguely. 'You two know each other, don't you? Surely you must know how he is?'

Part of her, the part that hurt the most, wanted to ask this intimidating woman how he was. If he was OK. If he was getting on with his life as if she'd never existed. She refused to let that want take hold.

Angela West ordered a skinny cappuccino and duly decided against eating anything. Was this what it was like when you spent your working life interviewing celebrities? Did you become weight-obsessed in the face of all that glossy gorgeousness?

'Unfortunately I can't really say we know each other,' she said. 'Shame, I'd love to have him on my Christmas card list. I only spoke to him the once. He was doing the publicity rounds for that film he'd just made, with the awards season looming. He mentioned he knew someone who worked for *Gossip!*—that was it.' She winked. 'Lucky you!'

A spike of uneasiness slipped unexpectedly into Jen's mind.

'Did he mention my article at all? My internship?' she asked, finding it hard to form the words because her mouth seemed suddenly dry.

'Which article was that, honey? Is it something on him? I could use a bit of extra background.'

Jen ignored the slight in that sentence, the implication that something *she* produced wouldn't be of any more value than 'background', because of the mounting feeling of cold awfulness in her stomach. She needed to clarify this. Right now.

'The article I wrote at the end of my internship. As part of my permanent job application. *How To Marry A Millionaire in Ten Easy Steps.*'

Angela laughed out loud. 'Good grief—is that the kind of thing they're commissioning now in the Features Department?'

The laugh wasn't light-hearted or friendly. Jen liked her less and less.

'No, honey, he never mentioned you really at all, except for saying he knew you and you worked here. Sorry.'

The catty flash in Angela's dark eyes gave away what she was thinking. *Starstruck kid, thinking Alex was into her.*

'Don't worry about the extra background if you don't know him that well. I'll call him up myself, cover some more ground.'

Jen barely noticed her sashaying away, tray in hand. She put her own tray down untouched on one of the empty tables on her way out.

She felt physically sick. She'd been so convinced he'd

swung the job for her and now it turned out he hadn't even mentioned her article. Dropping her name into conversation wasn't the same thing as pulling strings, was it? Would he have passed it off as nothing more than—what had her editor called it?—*networking*, if she'd given him the chance to explain? Which she hadn't. She was so prejudiced by her useless father that she hadn't wanted to listen.

What had she done?

Rule #10: If you do manage to land your millionaire, always, always agree to a pre-nup. This is your payment, your insurance that all your hard work will pay off. You weren't in it for love, anyway, right?

'I can't understand why you didn't let me come to stay with *you*,' Elsie grumbled for the hundredth time. 'We could have gone clubbing in London—maybe one of those clubs where the footballers go. We could have *really* washed that man right out of your hair. But instead you think pie and chips at the village pub is going to cut the mustard.'

She looked questioningly into Jen's face.

'I just fancied a quiet weekend away,' she said, because she had to say something. How could she tell Elsie that the job she'd aspired to for years now made her feel miserable and bitter. And that living in London, which had filled her with excitement while she did her internship, now felt lonely. The friends she'd made at *Gossip!* just reminded her of the mess she was in, cruising along rudderless because she now had no clue what she wanted from life.

Elsie waited, apparently for something more, then gave an exasperated snort and stood up.

'I'll get another round in. Might as well get plastered. There's nothing else to do.'

'I'll have a pint.'

Broken though it might be, Jen's heart was apparently still capable of beating crazily at the sound of Alex's voice, the sight of him.

Elsie's eyes were practically on stalks.

Hollywood Alex had come to Littleford. What a scoop that would be for the *Gazette*.

'Jen? Do you want to talk to him? Or shall I…?' Elsie paused, clearly fighting the urge to fall at Alex's feet. 'Get him out of here?'

Jen looked up at him. He looked tired, drawn.

Because of me, her mind whispered hopefully. She crushed the thought. He'd flown in from the States. He was jetlagged. It didn't mean anything.

'Elsie, could you give us a minute?' she said.

His green eyes held hers steadily and she suddenly re-alised Elsie hadn't moved an inch, apart from possibly dropping her jaw even wider.

'Elsie?' she hissed through gritted teeth.

'Hmm? Right. No problem. Leave you to it.'

Elsie backed reluctantly away towards the bar. Alex slid onto the bench opposite her.

'How did you find me?' she asked.

'I went to your house and your mum told me you were at the pub. There's only one in the village. It wasn't hard.'

She took a deep breath.

'Why are you here?'

'I want to make things right between us,' he said.

'Have you got a time machine?'

He didn't answer.

'I know you didn't pull strings,' she said. 'Not intention-ally, anyway. I want to tell you I'm sorry for not believing you, for thinking you'd undermine me like that, but when you didn't get in touch again I thought you'd just put us behind you and moved on.'

'I tried,' he said. 'But it didn't work.'

Her heart gave a half-skip but she ignored it. Nothing mattered now apart from making him understand.

'I've never criticised my mum for taking that payoff when I was a baby. She had her reasons. It meant she could buy the cottage in Littleford and at least not have to worry about having a roof over our heads. But it made me wary of anyone like my father, who has money and power, and it made me determined to make something of myself—an achievement that I could call my own, without help from anyone like that.'

'You wanted to prove that you never needed him, anyway?'

She gave a wry smile, thinking that somehow he'd managed to get closer to the hub of it all than she had.

'Yes, I suppose I did. And that's why I overreacted so badly. I thought you'd taken that chance away from me.'

'Jen—'

She held up a hand. 'Please. Let me finish. Let me explain.'

He leaned back against the bench.

'I found it hard at first to take any help from you, but then, as I got to know you, I began to realise there's a difference between offering help and trying to control someone. I should have trusted you and I'm so sorry that I didn't.'

'It's OK,' he said.

'Is it?'

He put a hand over hers and she felt sweet relief. Even if they couldn't go back to how things were, maybe at least she hadn't lost him altogether.

'It isn't your fault,' he said. 'I should have thought what it meant when I offered that interview. Just being connected with me opens doors—and I'm not saying that to be arrogant. It's just a fact. You're the first person I've come across that wanted those doors left shut.'

She gave a small smile. 'That makes me an idiot, doesn't it?'

'No, it makes you different. You've never wanted anything from me. It's never been about what publicity you could get, never a mutual benefit thing. When we're together it's about us, nothing else. All the help I gave you I had to bargain with you to take, and I loved that attitude. I would never have consciously screwed around with it and I'm truly sorry.'

The green eyes were full of remorse and her heart turned over softly.

'It's OK.'

'It isn't OK. After my divorce I fell into the habit of keeping control over every aspect of my life—to protect myself, I suppose. And because of that I messed with yours. None of this is down to you. It's the fallout from my damn marriage, and I should have let it go years ago.'

He squeezed her fingers.

'You saw what my family is like,' he said. 'There's never a dull moment, always someone to talk to. When I was a kid there was always someone to play with. I wanted that in my future, and that's what my marriage to Susan was about. I was building my work reputation up from scratch, giving it everything I had. It was all for us—for Susan and me and the family we'd have one day.'

He frowned.

'Things were easy at first, when we were both students. But when my career took off and I got serious studio backing that's when it started going wrong. I was away a lot and she didn't like it. Then when we were together things began to be strained. There was press interest even then. I was pictured out with people I worked with. There was never anything in it, but she just didn't have that level of trust in me that enabled her to let it go. By the time we broke up I'd made good money. I'd bought my parents that house, bought a place for us in London. I'd reached a point where I could start to pick and choose projects to work on. And then she took me to the absolute cleaners.'

'Maybe she thought she deserved a decent settlement,' Jen ventured. 'It can't have been easy with you away so much.'

'I offered her a decent settlement,' he snapped. 'It included the London house. But she got some good advice. She refused my offer and went to court to take as much as she could. I'd worked for that money from nothing. I'd poured my heart and soul into it to get where I was. And in one court judgement fifty percent of it was gone. Just like that.'

'It must have hurt.'

'I was furious. Absolutely livid for a very long time. I made the decision then that I wouldn't get involved again. That was it for me with relationships. If I couldn't trust someone who'd known me when I had nothing, how could I trust anyone?'

'But what about the family you wanted?'

He dropped his eyes briefly.

'That's what hurt the most. The papers went on about the financial cost of my divorce, but it cost me a lot more than that. If I couldn't give enough time and commitment to Susan because of my work, how the hell could I hope to make it work once children were thrown into the mix? My whole future crumbled when she left me the way she did.'

He looked back up at her, his gaze clear and unapologetic.

'So I made a new one. I was rich, I was successful, I had plenty of pretty girls crossing my path, so I decided to enjoy the bachelor party lifestyle without letting anyone get close. And for a while I thought I'd made the right decision. I had a scream of a time.' He paused. 'It's just recently that it's begun to feel like not enough.'

'Recently?'

'I began to wonder just who the hell I was slogging away like this *for*. And when I met you I began to understand.'

'Understand?'

'I'm still a family man underneath it all. Depriving myself of my family couldn't change that. For the first time in so long I started to think my life could be about more than just work. You make me want that, and if you give me a chance I promise we will always be an equal partnership. I will never do anything to undermine you again. I love you too much to want to restrict you.'

Jen was distracted from delicious shock at the fact he'd used the L-word by Elsie's gobsmacked gasp from across the bar as he put a tiny blue velvet box on the table in front of her.

'Is that...?'

'A proposal? Yes, it is. But before you say anything there's something I want to mention.'

She stared at the box on the table between them. In that box was the moment her life diverged. Two paths. One way with him. One way alone. And suddenly she knew what was coming.

The caveat.

She didn't blame him. She understood his reasons perfectly. And yet there was disappointment. That he thought she would be interested in half a fortune she'd had no part in earning and that her life was to be overshadowed by yet another contract. She'd thought he knew her better than that.

'You want to talk about a pre-nup,' she said.

He looked at her for a long moment.

'Why? Do you want one?' he asked.

She stared at him, unsmiling, and he dropped the light-hearted tone.

'You probably think a pre-nup is a given with me, right? Based on my past.'

She nodded slowly.

'Based on everything. You don't leave anything to chance, and that's something I'd have to try and work on if we were to go with this. Make you fly by the seat of your pants a bit more.' She offered him a smile. 'I don't blame you for being that way after what happened with your marriage.'

She glanced down again at the box in front of her. Give up Alex because of a principle? Could she do that? Her heart twisted at the thought of being without him again.

She could let all the prejudices her father had given her slide and just be with him. What did she care if there was a pre-nup, anyway? If they ever broke up she knew perfectly well she wouldn't want anything from him that she didn't deserve.

She could forgive him for giving *Gossip!* the interview, because despite all the angst and bitterness he hadn't swung the job for her. Not really. Just being connected to him opened doors, and if she wanted to be with him that was something she'd have to swallow however hard it stuck in her throat.

The choice was simple. She could be lonely and feel victorious or get rid of her stupid pride and be happy.

For him she would compromise. For *him*.

'*If* we were to go with this?' he said. 'How big is that "if" exactly?'

She took a deep breath.

'I love you,' she said. She saw his eyes light up at that

and it strengthened her resolve still further. 'I'm willing to sign a pre-nup, if that's what you want.' She paused. 'If that's what you need.'

He visibly tensed, and a light frown touched his face. Her hands were suddenly in his, surrounded by them.

'Thank you,' he said.

She smiled a little.

'But that won't be necessary.'

Her heartbeat jolted into action. She looked at him through narrowed eyes.

'What do you mean?'

'I'm guessing the thought of a monetary get-out-clause isn't something you want in your future, being as you have the one from hell in your past,' he said. 'So the answer is no, I won't be wanting a pre-nup. I don't intend to need one. I love you. I've never been more certain of anything.'

He lifted one hand to her cheek, stroked it gently. Heat sparkled along her cheekbone as if it might burst into flames. Her stomach did a slow and delicious cartwheel. She felt such love for him that it made her throat dry, and she knew tears might follow pretty soon if she didn't swallow hard.

'Jen, will you quit with all the questions and marry me?'

She waited a moment, just to let the full deliciousness of that question sink in and envelop her.

He got her.

It filled her with happiness. He lived his life with a safety net and he was letting that go. For her. Because he understood how important it was for her.

As he opened the box she looked down in awe at the square-cut diamond, yet nothing could have meant more than the trust he was putting in her.

'Yes,' she said, finally letting excitement bubble over. She wanted to jump up and down, leap around the bar.

He slid the ring on her finger, then held her hand tightly in his. He leaned forward to give her a hot kiss that made the locals gawp, and then something occurred to her. She put a hand on his shoulder, broke the kiss gently.

'Hang on,' she said. 'Didn't you say there were a few points you wanted to bring up before I gave you my answer?'

'I meant wedding details, you idiot. You can choose whatever you want—location, theme, guest lists. Anything. Just one condition.'

'What's that?'

'You have to include my family in there. I've got some bridges to build. Otherwise you get *carte blanche*. Marlon can do the styling, if you like. He really took to you.'

They both turned at the sound of exaggerated throat-clearing.

Elsie drew herself up to her full height.

'If there's any styling to be done,' she said, an indignant tilt to her chin, 'look no further.'

* * * * *

ROMANCE

A Ring to Secure His Heir	Lynne Graham
What His Money Can't Hide	Maggie Cox
Woman in a Sheikh's World	Sarah Morgan
At Dante's Service	Chantelle Shaw
At His Majesty's Request	Maisey Yates
Breaking the Greek's Rules	Anne McAllister
The Ruthless Caleb Wilde	Sandra Marton
The Price of Success	Maya Blake
The Man From her Wayward Past	Susan Stephens
Blame it on the Bikini	Natalie Anderson
The English Lord's Secret Son	Margaret Way
The Secret That Changed Everything	Lucy Gordon
Baby Under the Christmas Tree	Teresa Carpenter
The Cattleman's Special Delivery	Barbara Hannay
Secrets of the Rich & Famous	Charlotte Phillips
Her Man In Manhattan	Trish Wylie
His Bride in Paradise	Joanna Neil
Christmas Where She Belongs	Meredith Webber

MEDICAL

From Christmas to Eternity	Caroline Anderson
Her Little Spanish Secret	Laura Iding
Christmas with Dr Delicious	Sue MacKay
One Night That Changed Everything	Tina Beckett

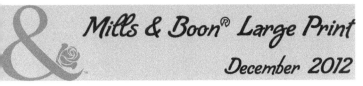

Mills & Boon® Large Print
December 2012

ROMANCE

Contract with Consequences	Miranda Lee
The Sheikh's Last Gamble	Trish Morey
The Man She Shouldn't Crave	Lucy Ellis
The Girl He'd Overlooked	Cathy Williams
Mr Right, Next Door!	Barbara Wallace
The Cowboy Comes Home	Patricia Thayer
The Rancher's Housekeeper	Rebecca Winters
Her Outback Rescuer	Marion Lennox
A Tainted Beauty	Sharon Kendrick
One Night With The Enemy	Abby Green
The Dangerous Jacob Wilde	Sandra Marton

HISTORICAL

A Not So Respectable Gentleman?	Diane Gaston
Outrageous Confessions of Lady Deborah	Marguerite Kaye
His Unsuitable Viscountess	Michelle Styles
Lady with the Devil's Scar	Sophia James
Betrothed to the Barbarian	Carol Townend

MEDICAL

Sydney Harbour Hospital: Bella's Wishlist	Emily Forbes
Doctor's Mile-High Fling	Tina Beckett
Hers For One Night Only?	Carol Marinelli
Unlocking the Surgeon's Heart	Jessica Matthews
Marriage Miracle in Swallowbrook	Abigail Gordon
Celebrity in Braxton Falls	Judy Campbell

Mills & Boon® Hardback

January 2013

ROMANCE

Beholden to the Throne	Carol Marinelli
The Petrelli Heir	Kim Lawrence
Her Little White Lie	Maisey Yates
Her Shameful Secret	Susanna Carr
The Incorrigible Playboy	Emma Darcy
No Longer Forbidden?	Dani Collins
The Enigmatic Greek	Catherine George
The Night That Started It All	Anna Cleary
The Secret Wedding Dress	Ally Blake
Driving Her Crazy	Amy Andrews
The Heir's Proposal	Raye Morgan
The Soldier's Sweetheart	Soraya Lane
The Billionaire's Fair Lady	Barbara Wallace
A Bride for the Maverick Millionaire	Marion Lennox
Take One Arranged Marriage...	Shoma Narayanan
Wild About the Man	Joss Wood
Breaking the Playboy's Rules	Emily Forbes
Hot-Shot Doc Comes to Town	Susan Carlisle

MEDICAL

The Surgeon's Doorstep Baby	Marion Lennox
Dare She Dream of Forever?	Lucy Clark
Craving Her Soldier's Touch	Wendy S. Marcus
Secrets of a Shy Socialite	Wendy S. Marcus

ROMANCE

Unlocking her Innocence	Lynne Graham
Santiago's Command	Kim Lawrence
His Reputation Precedes Him	Carole Mortimer
The Price of Retribution	Sara Craven
The Valtieri Baby	Caroline Anderson
Slow Dance with the Sheriff	Nikki Logan
Bella's Impossible Boss	Michelle Douglas
The Tycoon's Secret Daughter	Susan Meier
Just One Last Night	Helen Brooks
The Greek's Acquisition	Chantelle Shaw
The Husband She Never Knew	Kate Hewitt

HISTORICAL

His Mask of Retribution	Margaret McPhee
How to Disgrace a Lady	Bronwyn Scott
The Captain's Courtesan	Lucy Ashford
Man Behind the Façade	June Francis
The Highlander's Stolen Touch	Terri Brisbin

MEDICAL

Sydney Harbour Hospital: Marco's Temptation	Fiona McArthur
Waking Up With His Runaway Bride	Louisa George
The Legendary Playboy Surgeon	Alison Roberts
Falling for Her Impossible Boss	Alison Roberts
Letting Go With Dr Rodriguez	Fiona Lowe
Dr Tall, Dark...and Dangerous?	Lynne Marshall